The Writings of Owen Wister

THE PENTECOST OF CALAMITY
AND
A STRAIGHT DEAL

The Writings of Owen Wister

RED MEN AND WHITE

LIN McLEAN

HANK'S WOMAN

THE VIRGINIAN

MEMBERS OF THE FAMILY

WHEN WEST WAS WEST

LADY BALTIMORE

SAFE IN THE ARMS OF CROESUS

U. S. GRANT AND THE SEVEN AGES
OF WASHINGTON

THE PENTECOST OF CALAMITY AND
THE STRAIGHT DEAL

NEIGHBORS HENCEFORTH

The Writings of Owen Wister

of The American Academy of Arts and Letters

*Membre Correspondant de la Société
des Gens de Lettres*

Honorary Fellow of the Royal Society of Literature

The Pentecost of Calamity

and

A Straight Deal

PRINTED IN THE UNITED STATES OF AMERICA BY
R. R. DONNELLEY & SONS CO., AT THE LAKESIDE PRESS, CHICAGO

PREFACE—*"Pro-British!"*

EARLY in 1915, an invitation came from the president of Trinity College, Durham, North Carolina, to make the address at the commencement Exercises. I accepted, and set to work; and on June 9th following, delivered the address. The local paper at Raleigh expressed regret that some other speaker had not been selected, who could have talked about a more interesting subject. About a month later, the address was published in *The Saturday Evening Post,* and during the next month, August, 1915, with one or two additional paragraphs, written in consequence of a letter from Roosevelt, it came out as a small book, entitled *The Pentecost of Calamity.* It was an appeal to all Americans to wake up to the significance of the Great War.

Outside of Raleigh, North Carolina, it was found of interest in several places, being translated into French, Dutch, Italian, and Japanese; and reprinted in this country twenty-seven times. By the time that Americans did wake up to the significance of the Great War, the strain during our years of slumber had dealt death to our great and pa-

v

triotic ambassador to England, Walter Hines
Page. A noble son of North Carolina and an
old and affectionate friend of Woodrow Wilson, his published letters written during
those years between August 1, 1915, and
April 6, 1917, when Germany's bad guess
about us aroused us at last, are, because of
their very affection and their slow, reluctant
disillusion, the most tragic condemnation of
Wilson that I know.

A Straight Deal or *The Ancient Grudge*
followed *The Pentecost of Calamity*, first, as
a magazine article, while we were in the war,
and in 1920 as a book. This was written after
a journey through England and the battle
zone of France, undertaken as part preparation for the book in April, 1919. There had
been no idea of a book when the magazine
article was written; the idea came because of
the emphatic approbation and emphatic dis-
sent aroused by the article.

At that time, Americans had to give serious
reasons for sailing to Europe, or the State
Department refused them permission to do so.
It refused me. I was merely an author. Had I
been a banker—But to study conditions overseas 5 months after the Armistice, in order
to follow *The Pentecost of Calamity* by an-

other appeal to the American people, was not considered a serious reason by the State Department. It was so considered by the English Ambassador, Lord Reading. He didn't know what the nature of the appeal was to be, or indeed, that it was to be an appeal at all. But he knew *The Pentecost of Calamity;* and at his request the State Department issued me a passport.

It appealed to Lord Reading, I think, that a man on his own hook, at his own expense, financed by no magazine or newspaper, and without any backing but himself and his purpose, nothing but a private citizen, should be starting off to see the aftermath of war and tell his fellow citizens about it. It appealed to the people to whom I went in London and in Paris—Mr. Davis our ambassador, General Pershing, to mention but two. It opened important doors, provided military escort, got me a pitiful and overwhelming sight of France from the ruins of the Somme to those of the Meuse and the Moselle, and furnished me with the greatest memory of my life. I came back with two books in my head.

The first, *A Straight Deal,* was written during the following months, written in a sustained heat of grubbing up the true facts of our crises with Great Britain since our Independence, undistorted by politicians and school histories.

I preached a moral to my fellow-countrymen most unpopular to their inherited and carefully fostered hate of Great Britain. In fact, quite as consciously as when I wrote *Lady Baltimore,* I took the risk of making enemies. I did make some—but who were they? Mayor Hylan, of New York, and his breed; Mayor Thompson of Chicago, and his breed. Anybody, as Roosevelt says in his criticism of *Lady Baltimore,* can arrange some undeniable facts so as to produce a perfectly untrue, lopsided total. I showed by chapter and verse how our school histories had presented a lopsided Great Britain to young America. Well, I got off far more easily than I had expected. The book was excluded from certain public libraries where the Hylan-Thompson breed of voice has the say-so; an Irish hand wrote an entire pamphlet entitled, "Owen Wister, Anti-American," a number of German voices were raised against me, profuse with that easy, common stripe of wholesale, generalizing assertions without proof, that my history was false—and it all left my character spotted with an epithet

much in vogue: I was called "pro-British."
And it stuck.

"Probably," said the *Boston Evening
Transcript* no later than May 5, 1927,
"neither Sir Gilbert Parker nor Mr. Wister
would deny being pro-British."

Sir Gilbert, Canadian, probably wouldn't;
and I certainly can't, for I don't know what
it means. Are we at war with England?

What originally set me off, was the voice
of the man in the street, in 1917 and 1918,
while England and France every day were
fighting Germany, against whom we had also
declared war, but hadn't fought so much as a
skirmish after twelve months.

"What had England done in the war, anyway?" the man in the street kept asking.
Quite natural, and entirely patriotic for the
German secret agents among us to encourage
the man in the street to say this. They were
serving their country. But what was the
American doing? He was something more
than an imbecile, he was a verbal traitor,
for we and England were on the same side
against a common enemy. His silly, senseless
phrase, repeated like a sort of slogan, ended
by boring me, and I wrote the article of which
the book is a somewhat careful elaboration,

preaching the same moral, "Stop hating England."

Of course we hated England in 1776; of course the War of 1812 fed our hatred; of course the attitude of England in our Civil War was no cure for hate. Take that fact and put it with some other facts like it, suppress Samoa, suppress the Spanish War, suppress every occasion when England has befriended us, and you give young America a picture of Great Britain which any wholesome American boy most certainly ought to hate. Don't say a word to the boy about the various occasions on which France has been just as nasty to us as England, don't mention the fact that the French Emperor in 1862 wanted to recognize the Southern Confederacy as a nation, or that he sent over the hapless Maximilian to be Emperor of Mexico and a threat on our flank, while our Union was fighting for its life; just suppress all that and the boy will have a picture of a beautiful beneficent France, our eternal friend since Lafayette, which is precisely as distorted a likeness as the picture of a baleful bullying Britain, our eternal enemy since George the Third. That is the picture which the Thompson-Hylan breed would perpetuate if it can be done, and very naturally any book which spoils such a picture goes on their black list.

To keep on twisting the tail of the British Lion after 130 years, struck me as a sport which it was time for us to outgrow; some symptoms of intellectual maturity ought to be budding in a people numbering less than four million in 1790, but of more than 100 million in 1920; gigantic in energy, gigantic in resources, gigantic in everything except the habit of thinking. Why not start a little thinking outside your personal business, your groceries, your bonds, whatever it is you have to market, and that you want to persuade somebody to buy? Why not remember now and then that you are one among several important nations who have learned to think, and who do it quite often? What's your point *now,* at this time of day, when you have become a giant, in twisting the British Lion's tail as you did when you were a child? All this is why I grubbed away at *A Straight Deal,* and if all that is being ''pro-British''—let the Thompson-Hylans make the most of it!

But they will not make much. The whole business is too childish and silly to live for ever as an asset for the private ends of the Thompson-Hylans. It will dawn on the Ameri-

can mind some day that England has not been
our eternal enemy, any more than France has
been our perpetual friend; that self-preservation is the law which governs nations who
think, which shapes their policy toward each
other, according to what at each turn of affairs seems wisest for self-preservation. It
is because we did not think, that 1812 found us
utterly unprepared to fight England; it is because England had other war on her hands
that we didn't come to grief. It is because we
did not think, that 1917 found us utterly unprepared to fight Germany; it is because Germany had other enemies on her hands, that
she didn't come over and blow our skyscrapers sky high.

But hark in your ear: isn't this Thompson-
Hylan annexation of America by George V
something of a *mayor's nest?*

OWEN WISTER.

Long House, Bryn Mawr, 1928.

THE PENTECOST
OF CALAMITY

THE PENTECOST OF CALAMITY

Ever the fiery Pentecost
Girds with one flame the countless host.
—EMERSON.

I

BY various influences and agents the Past is summoned before us, more vivid than a dream. The process seems as magical as those whereof we read in fairy legends, where circles are drawn, wands waved, mystic syllables pronounced. Adjured by these rites, voices speak, or forms and faces shape themselves from nothing. So, through certain influences, not magical at all, our brains are made to flash with visions of other days. Is there among us one to whom this experience is unknown? For whom no particular strain of music, or no special perfume, is linked with an inveterate association? Music and perfumes are among the most potent of these evocatory agents; but many more exist, such as words, sounds, handwriting. Thus almost always, at the name of the town Cologne, the banks of the golden stream, the German Rhine, sweep into my sight as first I saw them long ago; and from a steamer's deck I watch again, and again count, a train composed of twenty-one locomotives, moving ominous and sinister on their new errand. That was July 19, 1870. France had declared war on Prussia that day. Mobilization was beginning before my eyes. I was ten.

Dates and anniversaries also perform the same office as music and perfumes. This is the ninth of June. This day, last year, I was in the heart of Germany. The beautiful, peaceful scene is plain yet. It seems as if I never could forget it or cease to love it. Often last June I thought how different the sights I was then seeing were from those twenty-one locomotives rolling their heavy threat along the banks of the Rhine. And, for the mere curiosity of it, I looked in my German diary to find if I had recorded anything on last June ninth that should be worth repeating on this June ninth.

Well, at the end of the day's jotted routine were the following sentences: "I am constantly more impressed with the Germans. They are a massive, on-going, steady race.

Some unifying slow fire is at work in them. This can be felt, somehow.'' Such was my American impression, innocent altogether, deeply innocent, and ignorant of what the slow fire was going to become. So were the peasants and the other humbler subjects of the Empire who gave me this daily impression; they were innocent and ignorant too. Therefore is the German tragedy deeper even than the Belgian.

On June twenty-eighth I was still in the heart of Germany, but at another beautiful place, where further signs of Germany's great thrift, order and competence had met me at every turn. It was a Sunday, cloudless and hot, with the mountains full of odors from the pines. After two hours of strolling I reentered our hotel to find a group of travelers before the bulletin board. Here we read in silence the news of a political assassination. The silence was prolonged, not because this news touched any of us nationally but because any such crime must touch and shock all thoughtful persons.

At last the silence was broken by an old German traveler, who said: ''That is the match which will set all Europe in a blaze.'' We did not know who he was. None of our party ever knew. On the next morning this party took its untroubled way toward France, a party of innocent, ignorant Americans, in whose minds lingered no thought of the old German's remark. That evening we slept in Rheims. Our windows opened opposite the quiet cathedral. It towered far above them into the night and sky, its presence filling our rooms with a serene and grave benediction. Just to see it from one's pillow gave to one's thoughts the quality of prayer.

Two days later I took my leave of it by sitting for a silent hour alone beneath its solemn nave. I can never be too glad that I bade it this good-by. Not long afterward— only thirty-two days—we recollected the old German's remark, for suddenly it came true. He had known whereof he spoke. On August 1, 1914, Europe fell to pieces; and during August, 1915, in a few weeks from to-day, the anniversaries will begin—public anniversaries and private. These, like perfumes, like music, will waken legions of visions. The days of the calendar, succeeding one another, will ring in the memories of hundreds and thousands like bells. Each date will invest its day and the sun or the rain thereof with special, pregnant relation to the bereft and the mourning of many faiths and languages. Thus all Europe will be tolling with memorial knells inaudible, yet which in those ears that hear them will sound louder than any noise of shrapnel or calamity.

II

Calamity, like those far-off locomotives on the Rhine, has again rolled out of Germany on her neighbors. Yet this very Calamity it is that has given me back my faith in my own country. It was Germany at peace which shook my faith; and I must tell you of that peaceful, beautiful Germany in which I rejoiced for so many days, and of how I envied it. Then, perhaps, among some other things I hope you will see, you will see that it is Germany who is, in truth, the deepest tragedy of this war.

The Germany at peace that I saw during May and June, 1914, was, in the first place, a constant pleasure to the eye, a constant repose to the body and mind. Look where you might, beauty was in some form to be seen, given its chance by the intelligence of man— not defaced, but made the most of; and, whether in towns or in the country, a harmonious spectacle was the rule. I thought of our landscape, littered with rubbish and careless fences and stumps of trees, hideous with glaring advertisements; of the rusty junk lying about our farms and towns and wayside stations; and of the disfigured Palisades along the Hudson River. America was ugly and shabby—made so by Americans; Germany was swept and garnished—made so by Germans.

In Nauheim the admirable courtyard of the bathhouses was matched by the admirable system within. The convenience and the architecture were equally good. For every hour of the invalid's day the secret of his wellbeing seemed to have been thought out. On one side of the group and court of baths ran the chief street, shady and well-kempt, with its hotels and its very entertaining shops; on the other side spread a park. This was a truly gracious little region, embowered in trees, with spaces and walks and flowers all near at hand, yet nothing crowded. The park sloped upward to a terrace and casino, with tables for sitting out to eat and drink and hear the band, and with a concert hall and theater for the evening. Herein comedies and little operas and music, both serious and light, were played.

Nothing was far from anything; the baths, the doctors, the hotels, the music, the tennis courts, the lake, the golf links—all were fitted into a scheme laid out with marvelous capability. Various hills and forests, a little more distant, provided walks for those robust enough to take them, while longer excursions in carriages or motor cars over miles of excellent roads were all mapped out and tariffed in a terse but comprehensive guidebook. Such was living at Nauheim. Dying, I feel sure, was equally well arranged; it was never allowed to obtrude itself on living.

Each day began with an early hour of routine, walking and water-drinking before breakfast, amid surroundings equally well planned—an arcade inclosing a large level space, with an expanse of water, a band playing, flowers growing in the open, cut flowers for sale in the arcade and comfortable seats where the doctor permitted pausing, but no permanent settling down. Thus went the whole day. Everything was well planned and everything worked. I thought of America, where so many things look beautiful on paper and so few things work, because nobody keeps the rules. I thought of our college elective system, by which every boy was free to study what best fitted him for his career, and nearly every boy did study what he could most easily pass examinations in. There was no elective system in Nauheim. Everybody kept the rules. There was no breakdown, no failure.

Moreover, the civility of the various ministrants to the invalid, from the eminent professor-doctor down through hotel porters and bath attendants to the elevator boy, was well-nigh perfect. If you asked for something out of the routine, either it was permitted or it was satisfactorily explained why it could not be permitted. Whether at the bank, the bookshop, the hotel, the railway station or in the street, your questions were not merely understood—the Germans knew the answers to them. And every day the street was charming with fresh flowers and fresh fruit in abundance at many corners and booths—cherries, strawberries, plums, apricots, grapes, both cheap and good, as here they never are. But the great luxury, the great repose, was that each person fitted his job, did it well, took it seriously. After our American way of taking it as a joke, particularly when you fumble it, this German way was almost enough to cure a sick man without further treatment.

III

This serenity of living was not got up for the stranger; it was not to meet his market that a complex and artificial ease had been constructed, bearing no relation to what lay beyond its limits. That sort of thing is to be found among ourselves in isolated spots, though far less perfect and far more expensive. Nauheim was merely a blossom on the general tree. It was when I began my walks in the country and found everywhere a corresponding, ordered excellence, and came to talk more and more with the peasants and to notice the men, women and children, that the scheme of Germany grew impressive to me.

So had it not been in 1870, as I looked back on my early impressions, reading them now in my maturer judgment's light. So had it not been even in 1882 and 1883, when I had again seen the country. We various invalids of Nauheim presently began to compare notes. All of us were going about the country, among the gardens and the farms, or across the plain through the fruit trees to little Friedberg on its hill—an old castle, a steep village, a clean Teutonic gem, dropped perfect out of the Middle Ages into the present, yet perfectly keeping up with the present. Many of the peasants in the plain, men and women, were of those who brought their flowers and produce to sell in Nauheim—humble people, poor in what you call worldly goods, but seemingly very few of them poor in the great essential possession.

We invalids compared notes and found ourselves all of one mind. Ten or twelve of us were, at the several hotels, acquaintances at home; every one had been struck with the contentment in the German face. Contentment! Among the old and young of both sexes this was the dominating note, the great essential possession. The question arose: What is the best sign that a government is doing well by its people—is agreeing with its people, so to speak? None of us were quite so sure as we used to be that our native formula, "Of the people, by the people, for the people," is the universal ultimate truth.

Twice two is four, wherever you go; this is as certain in Berlin as it is at Washington or in the cannibal islands. But, until mankind grows uniform, can government be treated as you treat mathematics? Until mankind grows uniform, will any form of government be likely to fit the whole world like a glove? So

long as mankind continues as various as
men's digestions, better to look at government as if it were a sort of diet or treatment.
How is the government agreeing with its people? This is the question to ask in each country. And what is the surest sign? Could any
sign be surer than the general expression, the
composite face of the people themselves? This
goes deeper than skyscrapers and other material aspects.

I had sailed away from skyscrapers and
limited expresses; from farmers sowing crops
wastefully; from houses burned through care-
lessness; from forests burned through care-
lessness; from heaps of fruit rotting on the
ground in one place and hundreds of men
hungry in another place. I had sailed away
from the city face and the country face of
America, and neither one was the face of
content. They looked driven, unpeaceful, dissatisfied. The hasty American was not looking after his country himself, and nobody
was there to make him look after it while he
rushed about climbing, climbing—and to
what? A higher skyscraper. It was very rest-
ful to come to a place where the spirit of man
was in stable equilibrium; where man's lot
was in stable equilibrium; where never a

schoolboy had been told he might become President and every schoolboy knew he could not be Emperor.

The students on a walking holiday from their universities often wandered singing through Nauheim. Somewhat Tyrolese in get-up, sometimes with odd, Byronic collars, too much open at the neck, they wore their knap-sacks and the caps that showed their guild. They came generally in the early morning while the invalids were strolling at the Spru-del. The sound of their young voices singing in part-chorus would be heard, growing near, passing close, then dying away melodiously among the trees.

A single little sharp discord vibrated through all this German harmony one day when I learned that in the Empire more chil-dren committed suicide than in any other country.

But soon this discord was lost amid the massive Teutonic polyphony of well-being. Of this well-being knowledge was enlarged by excursions to various towns. To Worms, for instance, that we might see the famous Luther Monument. Part of the journey thither lay through a fine forest. This the city of Frank-furt-am-Main owns and has forested for

seven hundred years; using the wood all the
time, but so wisely that the supply has main-
tained itself against the demand. I thought
of our own forests, looted and leveled, and of
ourselves boasting our glorious future while
we obliterated that future's resources. Frankfurt was there to teach us better, had we
chosen to learn.

IV

In Frankfurt-am-Main was born one of the
three supreme poets since Greece and Rome—
Goethe—from whom I shall quote more than
once; but Frankfurt has present glories that
I saw. It is one of many beautifully governed
German cities. I grew even fond of its Union
Station, since through this gate I entered so
often the pleasures and edifications of the
town. The trains were a symbol of the whole
Empire. About a mile north of Nauheim the
railroad passes under a bridge and curves
out of sight. The four-fifteen was apt to be
my express to Frankfurt. I would stand on
the platform, watch in hand, looking north-
ward for my train. At four-eleven the bridge
was invariably an empty hole. Invariably at
four-twelve the engine filled the hole; then
the train glided in quietly, and smoothly

glided on, almost punctual to the second. So did the other trains.

The conductors were officials of disciplined courtesy and informed minds. They appeared at the door of your compartment, erect, requesting your ticket in an established formula. If you asked them something they told you correctly and with a Teutonic adequacy that was grave, but not gruff. Once only in a score of journeys did I encounter bad manners. Now I should never choose these admirable conductors for companions, but as conductors they were superior to the engaging fellow-citizen who took my ticket down in Georgia and, when I asked did his train usually make its scheduled connection at Yemassee Junction, cried out with contagious mirth:

"My Lawd, suh, 'most nevah!"

In these German trains another little discord jarred with some regularity: the German passengers they brought from Berlin, or were taking back to Berlin, were of a heavy impenetrable rudeness—quite another breed than the kindly Hessians of Frankfurt.

We know the saying of a floor—that it is so clean "you could eat your dinner off it." All the streets of Frankfurt, that I saw, were clean like this. The system of street cars was lucid—and blessedly noiseless!—and their conductors informed with the same adequate gravity I have already noted.

I found that I developed a special affection for Route 19, because this took me from the station to the opera house. But all routes took one to and through aspects of municipal perfection at which one stared with envy as one thought of home.

Oh, yes! Frankfurt is a name to me compact with memories—memories of clean streets; of streets full of by-passers who could direct you when you asked your way; of streets empty of beggars, empty of all signs of desolate, drunken or idle poverty; of streets bordered by substantial stone dwellings, with fragrant gardens; of excellent shops; the streets full of prosperous movement and bustle; an absence of rags, a presence of good stout clothes; a people of contented faces, whether they talked or were silent—the same firm and broad contentment, like a tree deep-rooted, in the city face that was in the country face.

These burghers, these Frankfurters, seemed to be going about their business with a sort of solid yet placid energy, well and deliberately aimed, that would hit the mark at once without wasting powder. It was very different and very superior to the ill-arranged and hectic haste of New York and Chicago; here nobody seemed driven as though by invisible furies—the German business mind was not out of breath.

Such are my memories of Frankfurt at work. Frankfurt at leisure was to be seen in its Palm Garden. This was the town's place of general recreation; large, various, beautifully and intelligently planned; with space for babies to roll in safety, and there were the babies rolling, and their nurses; with courts for tennis, and thither I saw adolescent Frankfurt strolling in flannels and short skirts after business hours; with benches where sat the more elderly, taking the air and gazing at the games or the flowers or the pleasant trees; with paths more sequestered that wound among bowers, convenient for sweethearts—but I did not see any, because I forbore to look. A central building held tropic plants and basins, and large rooms for bad weather, I suppose, with a restaurant; but on this fine day the music played and we dined outside.

An entrance fee, very small, served to make

you respect the Palm Garden, since humanity seldom respects what it pays nothing for. Most unexpected show of all in this Palm Garden were the flowers under glass. I had erroneously supposed that any German scheme of color would be heavy, and possibly garish. Never had I beheld more exquisite subtlety on so extended a scale of arrangement. One walked through aisle after aisle of roses and other blooms in these greenhouses—everywhere was the same delicate sense and feeling; the same, in fact, in these flower schemes that one finds in German lyric verse, and in the songs of Schubert, Schumann and Franz.

It was in the opera house—Frankfurt has a fine and commodious one—that my whole impression of Germany's glory culminated. The performances drew their light from no Melbas or Carusos, or other meteors, but from a fixed constellation, now and then enriched by some visitor; it was teamwork of drilled and even excellence, singers, chorus, orchestra and scenery unitedly equal to the occasion, in operas old and new, an immense sweep of repertory, with an audience to match —an accustomed audience, to whom music was traditional food, music having always grown hereabout plenteously, indigenously, so that they took it as naturally as they took their Rhine wine, paying for it as moderately, going to hear it in rather plain clothes, as a rule—men in day dress, women in high-neck; not an audience that had to put on its diamonds in order to listen conspicuously to a costly and not comprehended exotic.

The difference between hearing opera where it grows and hearing it in New York is the difference between eating strawberries warm from their vines in June and strawberries in January that have come a thousand miles by freight. Where opera grows, it is the blend of native music, singers and listeners that gives a ripe flavor of a warmth which Fifth Avenue can never purchase.

This, every performance in Frankfurt had; but even this could be raised to a higher key of inspiration. I walked in one night and found myself amid a pious ceremonial. They were giving an old work, of bygone design, stiff in outline, noble, remote from all present things. Why did they revive this somewhat pale and rigid classic? For contrast, variety? Not at all. Two hundred years ago this day, Gluck had been born. Gluck had written this opera. For this reason, then, Frankfurt was assembled to hear Gluck's music and remember him; and, as I looked at these living Germans honoring their classics, I thought it was truly a splendid people that not only possessed but practically nourished themselves with these masterpieces of their great dead. But this was not all. This was Germany looking at its Past. In the Frankfurt opera house I also learned one of the ways in which Germany attends to its Future. It was on a Sunday afternoon. As I crossed the open space toward the opera house it seemed as though I were the only grown person bound there. Children by threes and fours, and in little groups, were streaming from every quarter, entering every door, tripping up the wide, handsome stairs, filling all the seats— boys and girls; it was like the Pied Piper of Hamelin. After a few minutes I found that I was indeed almost alone amid a rippling sea of children—nearly two thousand, as I later learned. In the boxes here and there was a parent or two with a family party, and dotted about the house a few scattered older heads among the young ones.

The overture began. ''Hush!'' went several little voices; the sprightly, expectant Babel fell to silence; they listened like a congregation in church.

Then the curtain rose. It was a gay old opera, tuneful, full of boisterous, innocent comedy and simple sentiment. Not Gluck this time; Gluck would have been a trifle severe for their young understandings. The enthusiasm and the attention of these boys and girls, with their clapping of hands and their laughter, soon affected the spirits of the singers as a radiant day in spring; it affected me. I envied the happy parents who had their children round them; it was like some sort of wonderful April light. Beneath it the quaint, sweet old opera shone like a fruit tree in blossom. The actors became as children again themselves; so did the fiddlers; so did the conductor. I doubt if that little old opera, *Czaar und Zimmermann,* had ever felt younger in its life; and I thought if the spirit of Goethe were watching Frankfurt, his city, to-day, it would add a new happiness to a moment of his Eternity.

Between the acts I was full of questions. What occasion was this? I read the program, wherein was set forth a most interesting account of the composer—his character, life and adventures, with a historic account also of Peter the Great, the hero of the opera; but nothing about the occasion. So in the lobby I addressed myself to a group of the men I had seen dotted among the rows of children. The men were schoolmasters. The occasion was an experiment. The children were of the public schools of Frankfurt—not the oldest scholars, but the middle grades of the schools. For the oldest, Frankfurt had already provided opera days, but this was the first ever given for these younger boys and girls. The cost was twelve-and-a-half cents a seat. If it proved a success, a second would follow in two weeks. At the theater, throughout each winter school term, plays were given expressly for them in this way—the great German classics; but never any opera before to-day.

Well, the performance went on; but I was obliged, near the end of it, to hasten away to my train for Nauheim, most reluctantly leaving the sight and company of those two thousand joyous children of the Frankfurt public schools. "Rosy cheeks predominated; eyeglasses were rare."—Again I quote from my own diary:—"The children seemed between ten and fifteen. The boys had good foreheads and big backs to their heads."

V

Nothing can efface this memory, nothing can efface the whole impression of Germany; in retrospect this picture rises clear—the fair aspect and order of the country and the cities, the well-being of the people, their contented faces, their grave adequacy, their kindliness; and, crowning all material prosperity, the feeling for beauty as shown by their gardens, and, better and more important still, the reverent value for their great native poets and musicians, so attentive, so cherishing, seeing to it that the young generation began early its acquaintance with the masterpieces that are Germany's heritage of inspiration.

Such was the splendor of this empire as it unrolled before me through May and June, 1914, that by contrast the state of its two great neighbors, France and England, seemed distressing and unenviable. Paris was shabby and incoherent, London full of unrest. Instead of Germany's order, confusion prevailed in France; instead of Germany's placidity, disturbance prevailed in England; and in both France and England incompetence seemed the chief note. The French face, alike in city or country, was too often a face of worried sadness or revolt; men spoke of

political scandals and dissensions petty and
unpatriotic in spirit, and a political trial, re-
vealing depths of every sort of baseness and
dishonor, filled the newspapers; while in England, besides discord of suffrage and discord
of labor, civil war seemed so imminent that no
one would have been surprised to hear of it
any day.

So that I thought: Suppose a soul, arrived
on earth from another world, wholly ignorant
of earth, without any mortal ties whatever,
were given its choice after a survey of the
nations, which it should be born in and belong
to? In May, June and July, 1914, my choice
would have been, not France. not England,
not America, but Germany.

It was on the seventh day of June, 1914,
that Frankfurt assembled her school children
in the opera house, to further their taste and
understanding of Germany's supreme national art. Exactly eleven months later, on
May 7, 1915, a German torpedo sank the *Lusitania;* and the cities of the Rhine celebrated
this also for their school children.

VI

The world is in agony. We witness the
most terrible catastrophe known to mankind

—most terrible, not from its huge size, but because it is a moral catastrophe. Through centuries of suffering and cruelty, guided by religion, we thought we had attained to knowledge of and belief in a public right between nations, and an honorable warfare, if warfare must be. This has been shattered to pieces. No need to investigate further the atrocities at Liège or Louvain. These and more have indeed been amply proved, but what need of proof after the Lusitania school festival? In that holiday we see the feast of *Kultur,* the Teutonic climax. How came it to pass? Is it the same Germany who gave those two holidays to her school children? The opera in Frankfurt, and this orgy of barbaric blood-lust, guttural with the deep basses of the fathers and shrill with the trebles of their young? Their young, to whom they teach one day the gentle melodies of Lortzing, and to exult in world-assassination on another?

Goethe said—and the words glow with new prophetic light: "Germans are of yesterday; ... a few centuries must still elapse before ... it will be said of them, 'It is long since they were barbarians.'" And again: "National hatred is a peculiar thing. You will always find it strongest and most violent where there is the lowest degree of *Kultur.*" But how came it to pass? Do the two holidays proceed from the same *Kultur,* the same Fatherland?

They do; and nothing in the whole story of mankind is more strange than the case of Germany—how Germany through generations has been carefully trained for this wild spring at the throat of Europe that she has made. The Servian assassination has nothing to do with it, save that it accidentally struck the hour. Months and years before that, Germany was crouching for her spring. In one respect the war she has incubated is the old assault of Xerxes, of Alexander, of Napoleon, of every one who has been visited by the dangerous dream of world conquest. Only, never before has the dream been taught to a people on such a scale, not merely because of the vast modern apparatus, but much more because no subjects of any despot have ever been so politically docile and credulous as the Germans.

In another respect this war resembles strikingly our own and the French Revolution. All three were prepared and fomented by books, by teaching from books. The American brain seized hold of certain doctrines and generalizations of Locke, Montesquieu, Burlamaqui and Beccaria concerning the rights of man and the consent of the governed. The French brain nourished and inspired itself with some theorems of the encyclopedists and of Rousseau about man's natural innocence and the social contract. The Teutonic brain assimilated some diplomatic and philosophic precepts laid down by Machiavelli, Nietzsche and Treitschke. Indeed, Fichte, during the winter of 1807–08, at the University of Berlin, made an address to the German people which may be accounted the first famous academic harbinger and source of the present Teutonic state of mind. Here the parallel stops. With America and France, war made way for independence, liberty and freedom, political and moral; Germany would establish everywhere her absolute military despotism. We shall reach in due course the full statement of her creed; we are not ready for it yet.

VII

Often of late I have thought of those twenty-one locomotives moving along the bank of the Rhine. They were a symbol. They stood for the House of Hohenzollern; they carried Cæsar and all his fortunes, which had begun long before locomotives were invented. July 19, 1870, is one of the dates that does not remain of the same size, but grows, has not done growing yet, will be one of History's enormous dates before it is done growing. The heavier descendants of those locomotives have been lugging to France a larger destruction, and more hideous, than their ancestors dragged there; but this new freight belongs to the same haul, forms part of one vast organic materialistic growth, and spiritual eclipse, of which 1870 and 1914 are important parts, but by no means the whole.

Woven with it is the struggle of nations for the possession of their own soul. Consider 1870 in this light: Through that war France took her soul out of the custody of an Emperor and handed it to the people; through the same war Germany placed her soul in the hands of an Emperor. Defeated France, rid of her Bonapartes; victorious Germany, shackled to her Hohenzollern! In the light of forty-five years how those two opposite actions gleam with significance, and how in the same light the two words *defeat* and *victory* grow lambent with shifting import! Unless our democratic faith be vain, France walked forward then, and Germany backward. But this did not seem so last June.

VIII

Had it not culminated before our eyes, the case of Germany would be perfectly incredible. As it stands to-day, the truly incredible thing is that she should have made her spring at the throat of an unexpecting, unprepared world. Now that she *has* sprung, the diagnosis of her case has been often and ably made—before the event, Dr. Charles Sarolea, a Belgian gentleman, made it notably; but prophets are seldom recognized except by posterity. The case of Germany is a hospital case, a case for the alienist; the mania of grandeur, complemented by the mania of persecution.

Very well do I remember the first dawning hint I had of this diseased mental state. It was Wednesday, August 5, 1914. We were in mid-ocean. Before the bulletin board we passengers were clustered to read that day's marconigram and learn what more of Europe had fallen to pieces since yesterday. This morning was posted the Kaiser's proclamation, quoting Hamlet, calling on his subjects "to be or not to be," and to defy a world conspired against them. In these words there was such a wild, incoherent ring of exaltation that I said to a friend: "Can he be off his head?"

Later in that voyage we sped silent and un-
lanterned through the fog from two German
cruisers, of which nobody seemed personally
afraid but one stewardess. She said:
"They're all wild beasts. They would send
us all to the bottom." No one believed her.
Since then we believe her. Since then we
have heard the wild, incoherent ring in many
German voices besides the Kaiser's, and we
know to-day that Germany's mania is anal-
ogous to those mental epidemics of the Middle
Ages, when fanaticism, usually religious, sent
entire communities into various forms of
madness.

The case of Germany is the Prussianizing
of Germany. Long after all of us are gone,
men will still be studying this war; and, whatever responsibility for it be apportioned
among the nations, the huge weight and bulk
of guilt will be laid on Prussia and the Hohenzollern—unless, indeed, it befall that Germany conquer the world and the Kaiser dic-
tate his version of History to us all, suppress-
ing all other versions, as he has conducted
the training of his subjects since 1888. But
this will not be; whatever comes first, this
cannot be the end. If I believed that the earth
would be Prussianized, life would cease to be
desirable.

To me the whole case of Germany, the whole process, seems a fatalistic thing, destined, inevitable; cosmic forces above and beyond men's comprehension flooding this northern land with their high tide, as once they flooded southern coasts; giving to this Teuton race its turn, its day, its hour of white heat and of bloom, its temperamental greatness, its strength and excess of vital sap, intellectual, procreative—all this grandeur to be hurled into tragedy by its own action.

The process goes back a long way behind Napoleon—who stayed it for a while—to years when we see the Germany of the Reformation, Poetry, Music, the grand Germany, blossoming in the very same moment that the Prussian poison was also germinating. About 1830, Heine perceived and wrote scornfully concerning the new and evil influence. This was a germination of state and family ambition combined, fermenting at last into lust for world dominion. It grows quite visible first in Frederick the Great. By him the Prussian state of mind and international ethics began to be formulated. By force and fraud he annexed weak peoples' territory. He cut Poland's body in three, blasphemously

inviting Russia and Austria to partake with
him of his Eucharist.
Theft has followed theft since Frederick's.
His cynical, strong spirit guided Prussia after
Waterloo, guided first the predecessor of Bismarck and next Bismarck himself, with his
stealing of Schleswig-Holstein, his dishonest
mutilation of the telegram at Ems and the
subsequent rape of Alsace and Lorraine in
1870. Very plain it is to see now, and very
sad, why the small separate German states
that had indeed produced their giants—their
Luthers, Goethes, Beethovens—but had always suffered military defeat, had been the
shambles of their conquerors for centuries,
should after 1870 hail their newly-created
Emperor. Had he not led them united to
the first glory and conquest they had ever
known? Had he not got them back Alsace
and Lorraine, which France had stolen from
them two hundred years ago? So they handed
their soul to the Hohenzollern. This marks
the beginning of the end.

IX

We can hardly emphasize too much, or sufficiently underline, the moral effect of 1870 on
the German nature, the influence it had on

the German mind. It is essential to a clear
understanding of the full Prussianizing
process that now set in. On the German's
innate docility and credulity many have dwelt,
but few on what 1870 did to this. Only with
Bismarck's quick, tremendous victory over
France as the final explanation is the abject
and servile faith that the Germans thence-
forth put in Prussia rendered conceivable to
reason. They blindly swallowed the sham
that Bismarck gave them as universal suffrage. They swallowed extreme political and
military restraint. They swallowed a rigid
compulsion in schools, which led to the excess
in child suicide I have mentioned. They swallowed a state of life where outside the indicated limits almost nothing was permitted
and almost everything was forbidden.

But all this proscription is merely material
and has been attended by great material welfare. Intellectual speculation was apparently
unfettered; but he who dared philosophize
about Liberty and the Divine right of Kings
found it was not. Prussia put its uniform
not only on German bodies but on their
brains. Literature and music grew corre-
spondingly sterilized. Drama, fiction, poetry
and the comic papers became invaded by a

new violence and a new, heavy obscenity. Impatience with the noble German classics was bred by Prussia. What wonder, since freedom was their essence?

Beethoven, after Napoleon made himself Emperor, tore off the dedication of his "Eroica" symphony to Napoleon. And Goethe had said: "Napoleon affords us an example of the danger of elevating oneself to the Absolute and sacrificing everything to the carrying out of an idea." Goethe fell frankly out of date in Berlin. Symphony orchestras could no longer properly interpret Mozart and Beethoven. A strange blend of frivolity and bestiality began to pervade the whole realm of German art. Scientific eminence degenerated *pari passu*. No originator of the dimensions of Helmholtz was produced, but a herd of diligent and thorough workers-out of the ideas got from England—like the aniline dyes—or from France—like the Wassermann tests—and seldom credited to their sources. So poor grew the academic tone at Berlin that a Munich professor declined an offer of promotion thither.

For forty years German school children and university students sat in the thickening fumes that exhaled from Berlin, spread everywhere by professors chosen at the fountain-head. Any professor or editor who dared speak anything not dictated by Prussia, for German credulity to write down on its slate, was dealt with as a heretic.

Out of the fumes emerged three colossal shapes—the Super-man, the Super-race and the Super-state: the new Trinity of German worship.

X

Thus was Germany shut in from the world. Even her Socialist-Democrats abjectly conformed. China built a stone wall, Germany a wall of the mind.

To assert that any great nation has in these modern days deliberately built around herself such a wall, may seem an extreme statement, and I will therefore support it with an instance—only one instance out of many, out of hundreds; it will suffice to indicate the sort of information about the world lying outside the wall that Germany has carefully prepared for the children in her schools. I quote from the letter of an American parent recently living in Berlin, who placed his children in a school there: "The text books were unique. I suppose there was not in any book

of physics or chemistry that they studied an
admission that a citizen of some other country had taken any forward step; every step
was by some line of argument assigned to a
German. As you might expect, the history of
the modern world is the work of German Heroes. The oddest example, however, was the
geography used by Katherine. (His daughter,
aged thirteen.) This contained maps indi-
cating the Deutsche Gebiete (the German
"spheres of influence" in foreign lands) in
striking colors. In North and South America
including the United States and Canada,
there are said to be three classes of inhabitants—negroes, Indians and Germans. For
the United States there is a black belt for negroes and a middle-west section for Indians;
but the rest is Deutsche Gebiete. Canada is
occupied mainly by Indians. The matter was
brought to my attention because one of Katherine's girl friends asked her whether she was
of negro or Indian blood; and when she replied she was neither her friend pointed out
that this was impossible for she surely was
not German. Information less laughable
about the morals taught in the German
schools I forbear to quote.

During forty years Germany sat within her

wall, learning and repeating Prussian incan-
tations. It recalls those savage rites where
the participants, by shouting and by con-
certed rhythmic movements, work themselves
into a frothing state. This has befallen Germany. Within her wall of moral isolation her
sight has grown distorted, her sense of pro-
portion is lost; a set of reeling delusions pos-
sesses her—her own greatness, her mission of
Kultur, her contempt for the rest of mankind,
her grievance that mankind is in league to
cramp and suppress her.

These delusions have been attended by
their proper Nemesis: Germany has misunderstood us all—everybody and everything
outside her wall.

Like the bewitched dwarfs in certain old
magic tales, whose talk reveals their evil without their knowing it, Germans constantly
utter words of the most naïf and grotesque
self-betrayal—as when the German Ambassador was being escorted away from England
and was urged by his escort not to be so down-
cast; the war being no fault of his. He answered in sincere sadness:

"Oh, you don't realize! My future is broken. I was sent to watch England and tell
my Emperor the right moment for him to

strike, when England's internal disturbances
would make it impossible for her to fight us.
I told him the moment had come.''

Or again, when a German in Brussels said
to an American:

''We were sincerely sorry for Belgium; but
we feel it is better for that country to suffer,
even to disappear, than for our Empire, so
much larger and more important, to be torpedoed by our treacherous enemies.''

Or again, when Doctor Dernburg shows us
why Germany had to murder eleven hundred
passengers:

''It has been the custom heretofore to take
off passengers and crew. . . . But a submarine . . . cannot do it. The submarine is a
frail craft and may easily be rammed, and
a speedy ship is capable of running away
from it.''

No more than the dwarf has Germany any
conception what such candid words reveal of
herself to ears outside her Teutonic wall—
that she has walked back to the morality of
the Stone Age and made ancient warfare
more hideous through the devices of modern
science.

Thus her Nemesis is to misunderstand the
world. She blundered as to what Belgium

would do, what France would do, what Russia would do; and she most desperately blundered as to what England would do. And she expected American sympathy.

Summarized thus, the Prussianizing of Germany seems fantastic; fantastic, too, and not of the real world, the utter credulity, the abject, fervent faith of the hypnotized young men. Yet here are a young German's recent words. I have seen his letter, written to a friend of mine. He was tutor to my friend's children. Delightful, of admirable education, there was no sign in him of hypnotism. He went home to fight. There he inhaled afresh the Prussian fumes. Presently his letter came, just such a letter as one would wish from an ardent, sincere, patriotic youth—for the first pages. Then the fumes show their work and he suddenly breaks out in the following intellectual vertigo:

"Individual life has become worthless; even the uneducated men feel that something greater than individual happiness is at stake, and the educated know that it is the culture of Europe. By her shameless lies and cold-blooded hypocrisy England has forfeited her claim to the title of a country of culture. France has passed her prime any-

way, your country is too far behind in its
development, the other countries are too
small to carry on the heritage of Greek culture and Christian faith—the two main com-
ponents of every higher culture to-day; so
we have to do it, and we *shall* do it—even if
we and millions more of us should have to
die.''

There you have it! A cultivated student, a
noble nature, a character of promise, Prussianized, with millions like him, into a gibber-
ing maniac, and flung into a caldron of blood!
Could tragedy be deeper? Goethe's young
Wilhelm Meister thus images the ruin of
Hamlet's mind and how it came about: "An
oak tree is planted in a costly vase, which
should have borne beautiful flowers in its
bosom; the roots expand and the vase is
shattered." Thus has Prussia, planted in
Germany, cracked the Empire.

XI

And now we are ready for the Prussian
Creed. The following is an embodiment, a
composite statement, of Prussianism, compiled sentence by sentence from the utter-
ances of Prussians, the Kaiser and his gen-
erals, professors, editors, and Nietzsche, part

of it said in cold blood, years before this war, and all of it a declaration of faith now being ratified by action:

"We Hohenzollerns take our crown from God alone. On me the Spirit of God has descended. I regard my whole . . . task as appointed by heaven. Who opposes me I shall crush to pieces. Nothing must be settled in this world without the intervention . . . of . . . the German Emperor. He who listens to public opinion runs a danger of inflicting immense harm on . . . the State. When one occupies certain positions in the world one ought to make dupes rather than friends. Christian morality cannot be political. Treaties are only a disguise to conceal other political aims. Remember that the German people are the chosen of God.

"Might is right and . . . is decided by war. Every youth who enters a beer-drinking and dueling club will receive the true direction of his life. War in itself is a good thing. God will see to it that war always recurs. The efforts directed toward the abolition of war must not only be termed foolish, but absolutely immoral. The peace of Europe is only a secondary matter for us. The sight of suffering does one good; the infliction of suffering does one good. This war must be conducted as ruthlessly as possible. "The Belgians should not be shot *dead*. They should be . . . so left as to make impossible all hope of recovery. The troops are to treat the Belgian civil population with unrelenting severity and frightfulness. Weak nations have not the same right to live as powerful . . . nations. The world has no longer need of little nationalities. We Germans have little esteem and less respect . . . for Holland. We need to enlarge our colonial possessions; such territorial acquisitions we can only realize at the cost of other states.

"Russia must no longer be our frontier. The Polish press should be annihilated . . . likewise the French and Danish. . . . The Poles should be allowed . . . three privileges: to pay taxes, serve in the army, and shut their jaws. France must be so completely crushed that she will never again cross our path. You must remember that we have not come to make war on the French people, but to bring them the higher Civilization. The French have shown themselves decadent and without respect for the Divine law. Against England we fight for booty. Our real enemy is England. We have to . . . crush absolutely

perfidious Albion . . . subdue her to such an
extent that her influence all over the world is
broken forever.

"German should replace English as the
world language. English, the bastard tongue
. . . must be swept into the remotest corners
. . . until it has returned to its original ele-
ments of an insignificant pirate dialect. The
German language acts as a blessing which,
coming direct from the hand of God, sinks
into the heart like a precious balm. To us,
more than any other nation, is intrusted the
true structure of human existence. Our own
country, by employing military power, has attained a degree of Culture which it could
never have reached by peaceful means.

"The civilization of mankind suffers every
time a German becomes an American. Let us
drop our miserable attempts to excuse Germany's action. We willed it. Our might shall
create a new law in Europe. It is Germany
that strikes. We are morally and intellec-
tually superior beyond all comparison. . . .
We must . . . fight with Russian beasts,
English mercenaries and Belgian fanatics.
We have nothing to apologize for. It is no
consequence whatever if all the monuments
ever created, all the pictures ever painted, all

the buildings ever erected by the great archi-
tects of the world, be destroyed. . . . The
ugliest stone placed to mark the burial of a
German grenadier is a more glorious monument than all the cathedrals of Europe put
together. No respect for the tombs of Shake-
speare, Newton and Faraday.

"They call us barbarians. What of it? The
German claim must be: . . . Education to
hate. . . . Organization of hatred. . . . Education to the desire for hatred. Let us abolish
unripe and false shame. . . . To us is given
faith, hope and hatred; but hatred is the
greatest among them."

XII

Can the splendid land of Goethe unlearn
its Prussian lesson and regain its own noble
sanity, or has it too long inhaled the fumes?
There is no saying yet. Still they sit inside
their wall. Like a trained chorus they still
repeat that England made the war, that Louvain was not destroyed, that Rheims was not
bombarded, that their Fatherland is the un-
offending victim of world-jealousy. When
travelers ask what proofs they have, the
trained chorus has but one reply: "Our government officials tell us so." Berlin, Cologne,

Munich—all their cities—give this answer to the traveler. Nothing that we know do they know. It is kept from them. Their brains still wear the Prussian uniform and go mechanically through the Prussian drill. Will adversity lift this curse?

Something happened at Louvain—a little thing, but let it give us hope. In the house of a professor at the University some German soldiers were quartered, friendly, considerate, doing no harm. Suddenly one day, in obedience to new orders, they fell on this home, burned books, wrecked rooms, destroyed the house and all its possessions. Its master is dead. His wife, looking on with her helpless children, saw a soldier give an apple to a child.

"Thank you," she said; "you, at least, have a heart."

"No, madam," said the German; "it is broken."

Goethe said: "He who wishes to exert a useful influence must be careful to insult nothing. . . . We are become too humane to enjoy the triumphs of Cæsar." Ninety years after he said this Germany took the Belgian women from their ruined villages—some of these women being so infirm that for months they had not been out-of-doors—and loaded them on trains like cattle, and during several weeks exposed them publicly to the jeers and scoffs and insults of German crowds through city after city.

Perhaps the German soldier whose heart was broken by Louvain will be one of a legion, and thus, perhaps, through thousands of broken German hearts, Germany may become herself again. She has hurled calamity on a continent. She has struck to pieces a Europe whose very unpreparedness answers her ridiculous falsehood that she was attacked first. Never shall Europe be again as it was. Our brains, could they take in the whole of this war, would burst.

But Calamity has its Pentecost. When its mighty wind rushed over Belgium and France, and its tongues of fire sat on each of them, they, too, like the apostles in the New Testament, began to speak as the Spirit gave them utterance. Their words and deeds have filled the world with a splendor the world had lost. The flesh, that has dominated our day and generation, fell away in the presence of the Spirit. I have heard Belgians bless the martyrdom and awakening of their nation. They have said:

"Do not talk of our suffering; talk of our glory. We have found ourselves."

Frenchmen have said to me: "For forty-four years we have been unhappy, in darkness, without health, without faith, believing the true France dead. Resurrection has come to us." I heard the French Ambassador, Jules Jusserand, say in a noble speech: "George Eliot profoundly observes that to every man comes a crisis when in a moment, without chance for reflection, he must decide and act instantly. What determines his decision? His whole past, the daily choices between good and evil that he has made throughout his previous years—these determine his decision. Such a crisis fell in a moment on France; she acted instantly, true to her historic honor and courage."

Every day deeds of faith, love and renunciation are done by the score and the hundred which will never be recorded, and every one of which is noble enough to make an immortal song. All over the broken map of Europe, through stricken thousands of square miles, such deeds are being done by Servians, Russians, Poles, Belgians, French and English, —yes, and Germans too,—the souls of men and women rising above their bodies, flinging

them away for the sake of a cause. Think of
one incident only, only one of the white-hot
gleams of the Spirit that have reached us
from the raging furnace. Out from the
burning cathedral of Rheims they were drag-
ging the wounded German prisoners lying
helpless inside on straw that had begun to
burn. In front of the church the French mob
was about to shoot or tear to pieces those
crippled, defenseless enemies. You and I
might well want to kill an enemy who had
set fire to Mount Vernon, the house of the
Father of our Country.

For more than seven hundred years that
great church of Rheims had been the sacred
shrine of France. One minute more and those
Germans lying or crawling outside the church
door would have been destroyed by the furi-
ous people. But above the crash of rafters
and glass, the fall of statues, the thunder of
bombarding cannon, and the cries of French
execration, rose one man's voice. There on
the steps of the ruined church stood a priest.
He lifted his arms and said:

"Stop; remember the ancient ways and
chivalry of France. It is not Frenchmen who
trample on a maimed and fallen foe. Let us
not descend to the level of our enemies."

It was enough. The French remembered France. Those Germans were conveyed in safety to their appointed shelter—and far away, across the lands and oceans, hearts throbbed and eyes grew wet that had never looked on Rheims.

These are the tongues of fire; this is the Pentecost of Calamity. Often it must have made brothers again of those who found themselves prone on the battlefield, neighbors awaiting the grave. In Flanders a French officer of cavalry, shot through the chest, lay dying, but with life enough still to write his story to the lady of his heart. He wrote thus:

"There are two other men lying near me, and I do not think there is much hope for them either. One is an officer of a Scottish regiment and the other a private in the uhlans. They were struck down after me, and when I came to myself I found them bending over me, rendering first aid. The Britisher was pouring water down my throat from his flask, while the German was endeavoring to stanch my wound with an antiseptic preparation served out to their troops by the medical corps. The Highlander had one of his legs shattered, and the German had several pieces of shrapnel buried in his side.

"In spite of their own sufferings, they were

trying to help me; and when I was fully con-
scious again the German gave us a morphia
injection and took one himself. His medical
corps had also provided him with the injection
and the needle, together with printed instructions for their use. After the injection, feeling wonderfully at ease, we spoke of the lives
we had lived before the war. We all spoke
English, and we talked of the women we had
left at home. Both the German and the Britisher had been married only a year. . . .

"I wondered—and I suppose the others
did—why we had fought each other at all. I
looked at the Highlander, who was falling to
sleep, exhausted, and, in spite of his drawn
face and mud-stained uniform, he looked the
embodiment of freedom. Then I thought of
the Tricolor of France and all that France
had done for liberty. Then I watched the German, who had ceased to speak. He had taken
a prayer book from his knapsack, and was
trying to read a service for soldiers wounded
in battle. And . . . while I watched him I
realized what we were fighting for. . . . He
was dying in vain, while the Britisher and
myself, by our deaths, would probably con-
tribute something toward the cause of civilization and peace."

Thus wrote this young French officer of

cavalry to the lady of his heart, the American lady to whom he was engaged. The Red Cross found the letter at his side. Through it she learned the manner of his death. This, too, is the Pentecost of Calamity.

XIII

And what do the women say—the women who lose such men? Thus do they decline to attend at The Hague the Peace Congress of foolish women who have lost nobody:

"How would it be possible, in an hour like this, for us to meet women of the enemy's countries? . . . Have they disavowed the . . . crimes of their government? Have they protested against the violation of Belgium's neutrality? Against offenses to the law of nations? Against the crimes of their army and navy? If their voices had been raised it was too feebly for the echo of their protest to reach us across our violated and devastated territories. . . ."

And one celebrated lady writes to a delegate at The Hague:

"Madam, are you really English? . . . I confess I understand better Englishwomen who wish to fight. . . . To ask Frenchwomen in such an hour to come and talk of arbitra-

tion and mediation and discourse of an armistice is to ask them to deny their nation. . . .
All that Frenchwomen could desire is to awake and acclaim in their children, their husbands and brothers, and in their very fathers, the conviction that defensive war is a thing so holy that all must be abandoned, forgotten, sacrificed, and death must be faced heroically to defend and save that which is most sacred . . . our country. . . . It would be to deny my dead to look for anything beside that which is and ought to be!—if the God of right and justice, the enemy of the devil and of force and crazy pride, is the true God.''

Thus awakened and transfigured by Calamity do men and women rise in their full spiritual nature, efface themselves, and utter sacred words.

If Germany's tragedy be, as I think, the deepest of all, the hope is that she, too, will be touched by the Pentecost of Calamity, and pluck her soul from Prussia, to whom she gave it in 1870. Thus shall the curse be lifted.

XIV

And what of ourselves in this well-nigh world-wide cloudburst?

Every man has walked at night through

gloom where objects were dim and hard to see, when suddenly a flash of lightning has struck the landscape livid. Trees close by, fences far off, houses, fields, animals and the faces of people—all things stand transfixed by a piercing distinctness. So now, in this thunderstorm of war, each nation and every man and woman is searchingly revealed by the perpetual lightnings. Whatever this American nation is, whatever aspect, noble or ignoble, our Democracy shows in the glare of this cataclysm, is even already engraved on the page of History, will be the portrait of the United States in 1914–15 for all time.

I want no better photograph of any individual than his opinion of this war. If he has none, that is a photograph of him. Last autumn there were Americans who wished the papers would stop printing war news and give their readers a change. So we have their photographs, as well as those of other Americans who merely calculated the extra dollars they could squeeze out of Europe's need and agony. But that—thank God!—is not what we look like as a whole. Our sympathy has poured out for Belgium a springtide of help and relief; it has flowed to the wounded and afflicted of Poland, Servia, France and Eng-

land. A continuous publishing of books, magazine articles and editorials, full of justice
and of anger at Prussia's long-prepared and
malignant assault, should prove to Europe
that American hearts and heads by the thousand and hundred thousand are in the right
place. Merely the stand taken by the *New
York Sun, New York Times, Outlook* and *Philadelphia Ledger*—to name no more—saves us
from the reproach of moral neutrality: saves
us as individuals.

Yet, somehow, in Europe's eyes we fall
short. The Allies, in spite of their recognition of our material generosity, find us spir-
itually wanting. In the *London Punch,* on the
sinking of the *Lusitania,* Britannia stands
perplexed and indignant behind the bowed figure of America, and, with a hand on her shoulder, addresses her thus:

In silence you have looked on felon blows,
  On butcher's work of which the waste lands
    reek;
Now, in God's name, from Whom your great-
    ness flows,
  Sister, will you not speak?

This is asked of us not as individuals but as
a nation; and as a nation our only spokesman

is our Government: "Sister, will you not speak?" Well—we did speak; but after nine months of silence. This silence, in the opinion of French and Belgian emissaries who have talked to me with courteous frankness, constitutes our moral failure.

"When this war began"—they say—"we all looked to you. You were the great Democracy; you were not involved; you would speak the justifying word we longed for. We knew you must keep out politically; this was your true part and your great strength. We altogether agreed with your President there. But why did your universities remain dumb? The University of Chicago stopped the mouth of a Belgian professor who was going to present Belgium's case in public. Your press has been divided. The word we expected from you has never come. You sent us your charity; but what we wanted was justice, ratification of our cause."

To this I have answered:

"First—Our universities do not and cannot sit like yours in high seats, inspiring public opinion. I wish they did. Second—We are not yet melted into one nationality; we are a mosaic of languages and bloods; yet, even so, never in my life have I seen the American press and people so united on any question. Third—Our charity is our very way—the only way we have—of telling you we are with you. I am glad you recognize the necessity of our political neutrality. Anything else would have been, both historically and as an act of folly, unprecedented. Fourth—Do not forget that George Washington advised us to mind our own business."

But they reply: "Isn't this your own business?" And there they touch the core of the matter.

Across the sea the deadliest assault ever made on Democracy has been going on, month after month. We send bread and bandages to the wounded; individually we denounce the assault. Columbia and Uncle Sam stand looking on. Is this quite enough? War being out of the question, was there nothing else? No protest to register? Did the wide ocean wholly let Columbia out? Europe, weltering in her own failure, had turned towards us a wistful look.

I cannot tell what George Washington would have thought; I only know that my answer to my European friends leaves them unconvinced—and therefore how can it quite satisfy me? Minds are exalted now, and white-hot. When they cool, what will our historic likeness be as revealed in the lightnings of this cosmic emergency? Will it be the portrait of a people who sold its birthright for a mess of pottage? Viewing how we have given, and the tone of our press, perhaps this would hardly be just. Yet I cannot but regret that we did not protest. What we lost in not doing so I see clearly; I cannot see clearly what we gained. We may argue thus in our defense: If it is deemed that we missed a great opportunity in not protesting as signatories of the violated Hague conventions, are not our proofs of the violations more authentic now than at the time? What we heard was incredible to American minds. We had never made or known such war. By the time the truth was established a protest might have seemed somewhat belated. Well, this is all the explanation we can offer. Is it enough?

It is too early to answer; certain it is that not as we see ourselves but as others see us, so shall we forever be. Certain it is also, and eternally, that through suffering alone men and nations find their greater selves. It is fifty years since we Americans knew the Pentecost of Calamity. These years have been

too easy. We have not had to live dangerously enough. We have prospered, we have
been immune, and our prosperity has proved
somewhat a curse in disguise.

In these times that uncover men's souls
and the souls of nations, has our soul come
to light, or only our huge, lavish body? In
1865 we had found our soul indeed. Where is
it gone? We have been witnessing many
"scholarly retreats," and every day we have
had to hear the "maxims of a low prudence."
Have they sunk to the core and killed it? God
forbid! But since August, 1914, we have stood
listening to the cry of our European brothers-
in-Liberty. They did not ask our feeble arm
to strike in their cause, but they yearned for
our voice and did not get it. Will History
acquit us of this silence?

Meanwhile, the maxims of a low prudence,
masquerading as Christianity, daily counsel
us to keep our arm feeble. It was not so that
Washington survived Valley Forge, or Lincoln won through to Appomattox. If the
Fourth of July and the Declaration it cele-
brates still mean anything to us, let our arm
be strong.

This for our own sake. For the sake of
mankind, if this war brings home to us that

we now sit in the council of nations and share directly in the general responsibility for the world's well-being, we shall have taken a great stride in national and spiritual maturity, and our talk about the brotherhood of man may progress from rhetoric towards realization.

XV

We have yet to find our greater selves. We have also to realize that Europe, since the Spanish War, has counted us in the concert of great nations far more than we have counted ourselves.

Somebody wrote in the *New York Sun:*

We are not English, German, Swede,
Or Austrian, Russian, French or Pole;
But we have made a separate breed
And gained a separate soul.

It sounds well; it means nothing; its sum total is zero. America asserts the brotherhood of man and then talks about a separate soul!

To speak of the Old World and the New World is to speak in a dead language. The world is one. All humanity is in the same boat. The passengers multiply, but the boat

remains the same size. And people who rock
the boat must be stopped by force. America
can no more separate itself from the destiny
of Europe than it can escape the natural laws
of the universe.

Because we declared political independence,
does any one still harbor the delusion that
we are independent of the acts and fortunes
of monarchs? If so, let him consider only
these four events: In 1492 a Spanish Queen
financed a sailor named Columbus—and Europe reached out and laid a hand on this hemisphere. In 1685 a French King revoked an
edict—and thousands of Huguenots enriched
our stock. In 1803 a French consul, to spite
Britain, sold us some land—it was pretty
much everything west of the Mississippi. One
might well have supposed we were independent of the heir of Austria. In 1914 they
killed him, and Europe fell to pieces—and
that fall is shaking our ship of state from
stem to stern. There may be some citizens
down in the hold who do not know it—among
a hundred million people you cannot expect to
have no imbeciles.

Thus, from Palos, in 1492, to Sarajevo, in
1914, the hand of Europe has drawn us ever
and ever closer.

Yes, indeed; we are all in the same boat. Europe has never forgotten some words spoken here once: "That government of the people, by the people, for the people, shall not perish from the earth." She waited to hear us repeat that in some form when The Hague conventions we signed were torn to scraps of paper. Perhaps nothing save calamity will teach us what Europe is thankful to have learned again—that some things are worse than war, and that you can pay too high a price for peace; but that you cannot pay too high for the finding and keeping of your own soul.

A STRAIGHT DEAL

TO

EDWARD AND ANNA MARTIN

WHO GIVE HELP IN TIME OF TROUBLE

. . . mihi parva rura et
Spiritum Graiae tenuem Camenae
Parca non mendax dedit, et malignum
Spernere vulgus.

TABLE OF CONTENTS

A STRAIGHT DEAL

or,

The Ancient Grudge

I

CONCERNING ONE'S LETTER BOX

PUBLISH any sort of conviction related to these morose days through which we are living, and letters will shower upon you like leaves in October. No matter what your conviction be, it will shake both yeas and nays loose from various minds where they were hanging ready to fall. Never was a time when so many brains rustled with hates and panaceas that would sail wide into the air at the lightest jar. Try it and see. Say that you believe in God, or do not; say that Democracy is the key to the millennium, or the survival of the unfittest; that Labor is worse than the Kaiser, or better; that drink is a demon, or that wine ministers to the health and the cheer of man—say what you please, and the yeas and nays will pelt you. So insecurely do the plainest, oldest truths dangle in a mob of disheveled brains, that it is likely, did you assert twice two continues to equal four and we had best stick to the multiplication table, anonymous letters will come to you full of passionate abuse. Thinking comes hard to all of us. To some it never comes at all, because their heads lack the machinery. How many of such are there among us, and how can we find them out before they do us harm? Science has a test for this. It has been applied to the army recruit, but to the civilian voter not yet. The voting moron still runs amuck in our Democracy. Our native American air is infected with alien breath. It is so thick with opinions that the light is obscured. Will the sane ones eventually prevail and heal the sick atmosphere? We must at least assume so. Else, how could we go on?

II

DURING the winter of 1915 I came to think that Germany had gone dangerously but methodically mad, and that the European War vitally concerned ourselves. This conviction I put in a book. Yeas and nays pelted me. Time seems to show the yeas had it.

During May, 1918, I thought we made a mistake to hate England. I said so at the earliest opportunity. Again came the yeas and nays. You shall see some of these. They are of help. Time has not settled this question. It is as alive as ever—more alive than ever. What if the Armistice was premature? What if Germany absorb Russia and join Japan? What if the League of Nations break like a toy?

Yeas and nays are put here without the consent of their writers, whose names, of course, do not appear, and who, should they ever see this, are begged to take no offense. None is intended. There is no intention except to persuade, if possible, a few readers, at least, that hatred of England is not wise, is not justified to-day, and has never been more than partly justified. It is based upon three foundations fairly distinct yet meeting and merging on occasions: first and worst, our school histories of the Revolution; second, certain policies and actions of England since then, generally distorted or falsified by our politicians; and lastly certain national traits in each country that the other does not share and which have hitherto produced perennial personal friction between thousands of English and American individuals of every station in life. These shall in due time be illustrated by two sets of anecdotes: one, disclosing the English traits, the other the American. I say English, and not British, advisedly, because both the Scotch and the Irish seem to be without those traits which especially grate upon us and upon which we especially grate. And now for the letters.

The first is from a soldier, an enlisted man, writing from France.

"Allow me to thank you for your article entitled 'The Ancient Grudge.' . . . Like many other young Americans there was instilled in me from early childhood a feeling of resentment against our democratic cousins across the Atlantic and I was only too ready to accept as true those stories I heard of England shirking her duty and hiding behind her colonies, etc. It was not until I came over here and saw what she was really doing that my opinion began to change.

"When first my division arrived in France it was brigaded with and received its initial experience with the British, who proved to us how little we really knew of the war as it was and that we had yet much to learn. Soon my opinion began to change and I was regarding England as the backbone of the Allies. Yet there remained a certain something I could not forgive them. What it was you know, and have proved to me that it is not our place to judge and that we have much for which to be thankful to our great Ally.

"Assuring you that your . . . article has succeeded in converting one who needed conversion badly I beg to remain. . . ."

How many American soldiers in Europe, I wonder, have looked about them, have used their sensible independent American brains (our very best characteristic), have left school histories and hearsay behind them and judged the English for themselves? A good many, it is to be hoped. What that judgment

finally becomes must depend not alone upon
the personal experience of each man. It must
also come from that liberality of outlook which
is attained only by getting outside your own
place and seeing a lot of customs and people
that differ from your own. A mind thus sea-
soned and balanced no longer leaps to an opinion about a whole nation from the sporadic
conduct of individual members of it. It is to
be feared that some of our soldiers may never
forget or make allowance for a certain insult
they received in the streets of London. But
of this later. The following sentence is from
a letter written by an American sailor:

"I have read . . . 'The Ancient Grudge'
and I wish it could be read by every man on
our big ship as I know it would change a lot
of their attitude toward England. I have ar-
gued with lots of them and have shown some
of them where they are wrong but the Catholics and descendants of Ireland have a different argument and as my education isn't very
great, I know very little about what England
did to the Catholics in Ireland."

Ireland I shall discuss later. Ireland is no
more our business to-day than the South was
England's business in 1861. That the Irish
question should defeat an understanding be-

tween ourselves and England would be, to quote what a gentleman who is at once a loyal Catholic and a loyal member of the British Government said to me, "wrecking the ship for a ha'pennyworth of tar."

The following is selected from the nays, and was written by a business man. I must not omit to say that the writers of all these letters are strangers to me.

"As one American citizen to another . . . permit me to give my personal view on your subject of 'The Ancient Grudge' . . .

"To begin with, I think that you start with a false idea of our kinship—with the idea that America, because she speaks the language of England, because our laws and customs are to a great extent of the same origin, because much that is good among us came from there also, is essentially of English character, bound up in some way with the success or failure of England.

"Nothing, in my opinion, could be further from the truth. We are a distinctive race—no more English, nationally, than the present King George is German—as closely related and as alike as a celluloid comb and a stick of dynamite.

"We are bound up in the success of America only. The English are bound up in the success of England only. We are as friendly as rival corporations. We can unite in a common cause, as we have, but, once that is over, we will go our own way—which way, owing to the increase of our shipping and foreign trade, is likely to become more and more antagonistic to England's.

"England has been a commercially unscrupulous nation for generations and it is idle to throw the blame for this or that act of a nation on an individual. Such arguments might be kept up indefinitely as regards an act of any country. A responsible nation must bear the praise or odium that attaches to any national action. If England has experienced a change of heart it has occurred since the days of the Boer Republic—as wanton a steal as Belgium, with even less excuse, and attended with sufficient brutality for all practical purposes. . . .

"She has done us many an ill turn gratuitously and not a single good turn that was not dictated by selfish policy or jealousy of others. She has shown herself, up till yesterday at least, grasping and unscrupulous. She is no worse than the others probably—possibly even better—but it would be doing our country an ill turn to persuade its citizens that England was anything less than an active, dangerous competitor, especially in the infancy of our foreign trade. When a business rival gives you the glad hand and asks fondly after the children, beware lest the ensuing emotions cost you money.

"No: our distrust for England has not its life and being in pernicious textbooks. To really believe that would be an insult to our intelligence—even grudges cannot live without real food. Should England become helpless to-morrow, our animosity and distrust would die to-morrow, because we would know that she had it no longer in her power to injure us. Therein lies the feeling—the textbooks merely echo it. . . .

"In my opinion, a navy somewhat larger than England's would practically eliminate from America that 'Ancient Grudge' you deplore. It is England's navy—her boasted and actual control of the seas—which threatens and irritates every nation on the face of the globe that has maritime aspirations. She may use it with discretion, as she has for years. It may even be at times a source of protection to others, as it has—but so long as it exists as a supreme power it is a constant source of danger and food for grudges.

"We will never be a free nation until our

navy surpasses England's. The world will never be a free world until the seas and trade routes are free to all, at all times, and without any menace, however benevolent.

"In conclusion . . . allow me to again state that I write as one American citizen to another with not the slightest desire to say anything that may be personally obnoxious. My own ancestors were from England. My personal relations with the Englishmen I have met have been very pleasant. I can readily believe that there are no better people living, but I feel so strongly on the subject, nationally—so bitterly opposed to a continuance of England's sea control—so fearful that our people may be lulled into a feeling of false security, that I cannot help trying to combat, with every small means in my power, anything that seems to propagate a dangerous friendship."

I received no dissenting letter superior to this. To the writer of it I replied that I agreed with much that he said, but that even so it did not in my opinion outweigh the reasons I had given (and shall now give more abundantly) in favor of dropping our hostile feeling toward England.

My correspondent says that we differ as a

race from the English as much as a celluloid
comb from a stick of dynamite. Did our soldiers find the difference as great as that? I
doubt if our difference from anybody is quite
as great as that. Again, my correspondent
says that we are bound up in our own success only, and England is bound up in hers
only. I agree. But suppose the two successes
succeed better through friendship than
through enmity? We are as friendly, my correspondent says, as two rival corporations.
Again I agree. Has it not been proved this
long while that competing corporations pros-
per through friendship? Did not the Northern
Pacific and the Great Northern form a combination called the Northern Securities, for
the sake of mutual benefit? Under the Sherman Act the Northern Securities was dissolved; but no Sherman act forbids a Liberty
Securities. Liberty, defined and assured by
Law, is England's gift to the modern world.
Liberty, defined and assured by Law, is the
central purpose of our Constitution. Just as
identically as the Northern Pacific and Great
Northern run from St. Paul to Seattle do
England and the United States aim at Liberty, defined and assured by Law. As friends,
the two nations can swing the world towards

world stability. My correspondent would hardly have instanced the Boers in his reference to England's misdeeds, had he reflected upon the part the Boers have played in England's struggle with Germany.

I will point out no more of the latent weaknesses that underlie various passages in this letter, but proceed to the remaining letters that I have selected. I gave one from an enlisted man and one from a sailor; this is from a commissioned officer, in France.

"I cannot refrain from sending you a line of appreciation and thanks for giving the people at home a few facts that I am sure some do not know and throwing a light upon a much discussed topic, which I am sure will help to remove from some of their minds a foolish bigoted antipathy."

Upon the single point of our school histories of the Revolution, some of which I had named as being guilty of distorting the facts, a correspondent writes from Nebraska:

"Some months ago . . . the question came to me, what about our Montgomery's History now. . . . I find that everywhere it is *the King* who is represented as taking these measures against the American people. On page 134 is the heading, *American Commerce;*

the new King, George III; how he interfered with trade; page 135, *The King proposes to tax the Colonies;* page 136, 'The best men in Parliament—such men as William Pitt and Edmund Burke—took the side of the colonies.' On page 138, 'William Pitt said in Parliament, "in my opinion, this kingdom has no right to lay a tax on the colonies . . . I rejoice that America has resisted" '; page 150, 'The English people would not volunteer to fight the Americans and the King had to hire nearly 30,000 Hessians to help do the work. . . . The Americans had not sought separation; the King—not the English people—had forced it on them. . . .'

"I am writing this . . . because, as I was glad to see, you did not mince words in naming several of the worse offenders." (He means certain school histories that I mentioned and shall mention later again.)

An official from Pittsburgh wrote thus:

"In common with many other people, I have had the same idea that England was not doing all she could in the war, that while her colonies were in the thick of it, she, herself, seemed to be sparing herself, but after reading this article . . . I will frankly and candidly confess to you that it has changed my opinion, made me a strong supporter of England, and above all made me a better American.''

From Massachusetts:

"It is well to remind your readers of the errors—or worse—in American school text books and to recount Britain's achievements in the present war. But of what practical avail are these things when a man so highly placed as the present Secretary of the Navy asks a Boston audience (Tremont Temple, October 30, 1918) to believe that it was the American navy which made possible the transportation of over 2,000,000 Americans to France without the loss of a single transport on the way over? Did he not know that the greater part of those troops were not only transported, but convoyed, by British vessels, largely withdrawn for that purpose from such vital service as the supply of food to Britain's civil population?''

The omission on the part of our Secretary of the Navy was later quietly rectified by an official publication of the British Government, wherein it appeared that some sixty per cent of our troops were transported in British ships. Our Secretary's regrettable slight to our British allies was immediately set right by Admiral Sims, who forthwith, both in public and in private, paid full and appreciative tribute to what had been done. It is, nevertheless, very likely that some Americans will learn here for the first time that more than half of our troops were not transported by ourselves, and could not have been transported at all but for British assistance. There are many persons who still believe what our politicians and newspapers tell them. No incident that I shall relate further on serves better to point the chief international moral at which I am driving throughout these pages, and at which I have already hinted: Never to generalize the character of a whole nation by the acts of individual members of it. That is what everybody does, ourselves, the English, the French, everybody. You can form no valid opinion of any nation's characteristics, not even your own, until you have met hundreds of its people, men and women, and had ample opportunity to observe and know them beneath the surface. Here on the one hand we had our Secretary of the Navy. He gave our Navy the whole credit for getting our soldiers overseas. He justified the British opinion that we are a nation of braggarts. On the other hand, in London, we had Admiral Sims, another American, a splendid antidote. He corrected the Secretary's brag. What is the moral? Look out how you generalize. Since we entered the war that tribe of English has increased who judge us with an open mind, discriminate between us, draw close to a just appraisal of our qualities and defects, and possibly even discern that those who fill our public positions are mostly on a lower level than those who elect them.

I proceed with two more letters, both dissenting, and both giving very typically, as it seems to me, the American feeling about England—partially justified by instances mentioned by my correspondent, but equally mentioned by me in passages which he seems to have skipped.

"Lately I read and did not admire your article . . . 'The Ancient Grudge.' Many of your statements are absolutely true, and I recognize the fact that England's help in this war has been invaluable. Let it go at that and hush!

"I do not defend our own Indian policy. . . . Wounded and disabled in our Indian wars . . . I know all about them and how indefensible they are. . . .

"England has been always our only legiti-

mate enemy. 1776? Yes, call it ancient history and forget it if possible. 1812? That
may go in the same category. But the causes
of that misunderstanding were identically repeated in 1914 and '15.

"1861? Is that also ancient? Perhaps—
but very bitter in the memory of many of us
now living. The *Alabama*. The Confederate
Commissioners (I know you will say we were
wrong there—and so we may have been tech-
nically—but John Bull bullied us into compli-
ance when our hands were tied). Lincoln told
his Cabinet 'one war at a time, Gentlemen'
and submitted. . . .

"In 1898 we were a strong and powerful
nation and a dangerous enemy to provoke.
England recognized the fact and acted accordingly. England entered the present war to
protect small nations! Heaven save the mark!
You surely read your history. Pray tell me
something of England's policy in South Africa, India, the Soudan, Persia, Abyssinia,
Ireland, Egypt. The lost provinces of Denmark. The United States when she was young
and helpless. And thus, almost to infinitum.

"Do you not know that the foundations of
ninety per cent of the great British fortunes
came from the loot of India? upheld and

fostered by the great and unscrupulous East
India Company? . . .

"Come down to later times: to-day for instance. Here in California . . . I meet and
associate with hundreds of Britishers. Are
they American citizens? I had almost said,
'No, not one.' Sneering and contemptuous of
America and American institutions. Continu-
ally finding fault with our government and
our people. Comparing these things with
England, always to our disadvantage. . . .

"Now do you wonder we do not like England? Am I pro-German? I should laugh
and so would you if you knew me."

To this correspondent I did not reply that
I wished I knew him—which I do—that, even
as he, so I had frequently been galled by the
rudeness and the patronizing of various speci-
mens, high and low, of the English race. But
something I did reply, to the effect that I
asked nobody to consider England flawless, or
any nation a charitable institution, but merely
to be fair, and to consider a cordial understanding between us greatly to our future advantage. To this he answered, in part, as
follows:

"I wish to thank you for your kindly reply.
. . . Your argument is that as a matter of

policy we should conciliate Great Britain.
Have we fallen so low, this great and powerful nation? . . . Truckling to some other
power because its backing, moral or physical,
may some day be of use to us, even tho' we
know that in so doing we are surrendering
our dearest rights, principles, and dignity!
. . . Oh! my dear Sir, you surely do not advo-
cate this? I inclose an editorial clipping. . . .
Is it no shock to you when Winston Churchill
shouts to High Heaven that under no circumstances will Great Britain surrender its supreme control of the seas? This in reply to
President Wilson's plea for freedom of the
seas and curtailment of armaments. . . . But
as you see, our President and our Mr. Daniels
have already said, 'Very well, we will out-
build you.' Never again shall Great Britain
stop our mail ships and search our private
mails. Already has England declared an em-
bargo against our exports in many essential
lines and already are we expressing our
dissatisfaction and taking means to re-
taliate. . . .''

Of the editorial clipping inclosed with the
above, the following is a part:

''John Bull is our associate in the contest
with the Kaiser. There is no doubt as to his

position on that proposition. He went after
the Dutch in great shape. Next to France he
led the way and said, 'Come on, Yanks; we
need your help. We will put you in the first
line of trenches where there will be good gun-
ning. Yes, we will do all of that and at the
same time we will borrow your money, raised
by Liberty Loans, and use it for the purchase
of American wheat, pork, and beef.'

"Mr. Bull kept his word. He never flinched
or attempted to dodge the issue. He kept
strictly in the middle of the road. His deter-
mination to down the Kaiser with American
men, American money, and American food
never abated for a single day during the conflict."

This editorial has many twins throughout
the country. I quote it for its value as a
specimen of that sort of journalistic and political utterance amongst us, which is as seriously embarrassed by facts as a skunk by
its tail. Had its author said: "The Declaration of Independence was signed by Christo-
pher Columbus on Washington's birthday
during the siege of Vicksburg in the presence
of Queen Elizabeth and Judas Iscariot," his
statement would have been equally veracious,
and more striking.

As to Winston Churchill's declaration that Great Britain will not surrender her control of the seas, I am as little shocked by that as I should be were our Secretary of the Navy to declare that in no circumstances would we give up control of the Panama Canal. The Panama Canal is our carotid artery, Great Britain's navy is her jugular vein. It is her jugular vein in the mind of her people, regardless of that new apparition, the submarine. I was not shocked that Great Britain should decline Mr. Wilson's invitation that she cut her jugular vein; it was the invitation which kindled my emotions; but these were of a less serious kind.

The last letter that I shall give is from an American citizen of English birth.

"As a boy at school in England, I was taught the history of the American Revolution as J. R. Green presents it in his *Short History of the English People.* The gist of this record, as you doubtless recollect, is that George III being engaged in the attempt to destroy what there then was of political freedom and representative government in England, used the American situation as a means to that end; that the English people, in so far as their voice could make itself heard, were solidly against both his English and American policy, and that the triumph of America contributed in no small measure to the salvation of those institutions by which the evolution of England towards complete democracy was made possible. Washington was held up to us in England not merely as a great and good man, but as an heroic leader, to whose courage and wisdom the English as well as the American people were eternally indebted. . . .

"Pray forgive so long a letter from a stranger. It is prompted . . . by a sense of the illimitable importance, not only for America and Britain, but for the entire world, of these two great democratic peoples knowing each other as they really are and coöperating as only they can coöperate to establish and maintain peace on just and permanent foundations."

III

THERE, then, are ten letters of the fifty which came to me in consequence of what I wrote in May, 1918, which was published in the *American Magazine* for the following November. Ten will do. To read the other forty would change no impression conveyed already by the ten, but would merely repeat it. With varying phraseology their writers either think we have hitherto misjudged England and that my facts are to the point, or they express the stereotyped American antipathy to England and treat my facts as we mortals mostly do when facts are embarrassing—side-step them. What best pleased me was to find that soldiers and sailors agreed with me, and not "high-brows" only.

May, 1918, as you will remember, was a very dark hour. We had come into the war, had been in for a year; but events had not yet taken us out of the well-nigh total eclipse flung upon our character by those blighting words, "there is such a thing as being too

proud to fight.'' The British had been told
by their general that they were fighting with
their backs to the wall. Since March 23d the
tread of the Hun had been coming steadily
nearer to Paris. Belleau Wood and Château-
Thierry had not yet struck the true ring from
our metal and put into the hands of Foch
the one further weapon that he needed.
French *moral* was burning very low and blue.
Yet even in such an hour, people apparently
American and apparently grown up, were
talking against England, our ally. Then and
thereafter, even as to-day, they talked against
her as they had been talking since August,
1914, as I had heard them again and again,
indoors and out, as I heard a man one forenoon in a crowd during the earlier years of
the war, the miserable years before we waked
from our trance of neutrality, while our
chosen leaders were still misleading us.

Do you remember those unearthly years?
The explosions, the plots, the spies, the *Lusitania,* the notes, Mr. Bryan, von Bernstorff,
half our country—oh, more than half!—in-
different or incredulous, nothing prepared,
nothing done, no step taken, Theodore Roosevelt's and Leonard Wood's almost the only
voices warning us what was bound to happen,
and to get ready for it? Do you remember

the bulletin boards? Did you grow, as I did,
so restless that you would step out of your
office to see if anything new had happened
during the last sixty minutes—would stop as
you went to lunch and stop as you came back?
We knew from the faces of our friends what
our own faces were like. In company we
pumped up liveliness, but in the street, alone
with our apprehensions—do you remember?
For our future's sake may everybody remember, may nobody forget!

What the news was upon a certain forenoon
memorable to me, I do not recall, and this is
of no consequence; good or bad, the stream
of by-passers clotted thickly to read it as the
man chalked it line upon line across the bulletin board. Citizens who were in haste stepped
off the curb to pass round since they could not
pass through this crowd of gazers. Thus on
the sidewalk stood some fifty of us, staring at
names we had never known until a little while
ago, Béthincourt, Malancourt, perhaps, or
Montfaucon, or Roisel; French names of
small places, among whose crumbled, feature-
less dust I have walked since, where lived
peacefully a few hundred or a few thousand
that are now a thousand butchered or broken-
hearted. Through me ran once again the wonder that had often chilled me since the abdica-

tion of the Czar which made certain the crumbling of Russia: after France, was our turn coming? Should our fields, too, be sown with bones, should our little towns among the orchards and the corn fall in ashes amongst which broken hearts would wander in search of some surviving stick of property? I had learned to know that a long while before the war the eyes of the Hun, the bird of prey, had been fixed upon us as a juicy morsel. He had written it, he had said it. Since August, 1914, these Pan-German schemes had been leaking out for all who chose to understand them. A great many did not so choose. The Hun had wanted us and planned to get us, and now more than ever before, because he intended that we should pay his war bills. Let him once get by England and his sword would cut through our fat, defenseless carcass like a knife through cheese.

A voice arrested my reverie, a voice close by in the crowd. It said, "Well, I like the French. But I'll not cry much if England gets hers. What's England done in this war, anyway?"

"Her fleet's keeping the Kaiser out of your front yard, for one thing," retorted another voice.

With assurance slightly wobbling and a

touch of the nasal whine, the first speaker protested, "Well, look what George III done to us. Bad as any Kaiser."

"Aw, get your facts straight!" It was said with scornful force. "Don't you know George III was a German? Don't you know it was Hessians—they're Germans—he hired to come over here and kill Americans and do his dirty work for him? And his Germans did the same dirty work the Kaiser's are doing now. We've got a letter written after the battle of Long Island by a member of our family they took prisoner there. And they stripped him and they stole his things and they beat him down with the butts of their guns—after he had surrendered, mind—when he was surrendered and naked, and when he was down they beat him some more. That's Germans for you. Only they've been getting worse while the rest of the world's been getting better. Get your facts straight, man."

A number of us were now listening to this, and I envied the historian his ingenious promptness—I have none—and I hoped for more of this timely debate. But debate was over. The anti-Englishman faded to silence. Either he was out of facts to get straight, or lacked what is so pithily termed "comeback." The latter, I incline to think; for come-back needs no facts, it is a self-feeder, and its entire absence in the anti-Englishman looks as if he had been a German. Germans do not come back when it goes against them, they bleat "Kamerad!"—or disappear. Perhaps this man was a spy—a poor one, to be sure— yet doing his best for his Kaiser: slinking about, peeping, listening, trying to wedge the Allies apart, doing his little bit towards making friends enemies, just as his breed has worked to set enmity between ourselves and Japan, ourselves and Mexico, France and England, France and Italy, England and Russia, between everybody and everybody else all the world over, in the sacred name and for the sacred sake of the Kaiser. Thus has his breed, since we occupied Coblenz, run to the French soldiers with lies about us and then run to us with lies about the French soldiers, overlooking in its providential stupidity the fact that we and the French would inevitably compare notes. Thus too is his breed, at the moment I write these words, infesting and poisoning the earth with a propaganda that remains as coherent and as systematically directed as ever it was before the papers began to assure us that there was nothing left of the Hohenzollern government.

IV

"YOU will desire to know," said the Kaiser to his council at Potsdam in June, 1908, after the successful testing of the first Zeppelin, "how the hostilities will be brought about. My army of spies scattered over Great Britain and France, as it is over North and South America, will take good care of that. Even now I rule supreme in the United States, where three million voters do my bidding at the Presidential elections."

Yes, they did his bidding; there, and elsewhere too. They did it at other elections as well. Do you remember the mayor they tried to elect in Chicago? and certain members of Congress? and certain manufacturers and bankers? They did his bidding in our newspapers, our public schools, and from the pulpit. Certain localities in one of the river counties of Iowa (for instance) were spots of German treason to the United States. The "exchange professors" that came from Berlin to Harvard and other universities were so many camouflaged spies. Certain prominent

American citizens, dined and wined and flat-
tered by the Kaiser for his purpose, women
as well as men, came back here mere Kaiser-
puppets, hypnotized by royalty. His bidding
was done in as many ways as would fill a book.
Shopkeepers did it, servants did it, Americans
among us were decorated by him for doing
it. Even after the Armistice, a school text-
book "got by" the Board of Education in a
western state, wherein our boys and girls
were to be taught a German version—a Kaiser version—of Germany. Somebody protested, and the board explained that it
"hadn't noticed," and the book was held up.

We cannot, I fear, order the school histories in Germany to be edited by the Allies.
German school children will grow up believing, in all probability, that bombs were
dropped near Nürnberg in July, 1914, that
German soil was invaded, that the Fatherland
fought a war of defense; they will certainly
be nourished by lies in the future as they were
nourished by lies in the past. But we can prevent Germans or pro-Germans from writing
our own school histories; we can prevent that
"army of spies" of which the Kaiser boasted
to his council at Potsdam in June, 1908, from
continuing its activities among us now and

henceforth; and we can prevent our school textbooks from playing into Germany's hand by teaching hate of England to our boys and girls. Beside the sickening silliness which still asks, "What has England done in the war?" is a silliness still more sickening which says, "Germany is beaten. Let us forgive and forget." That is not Christianity. There is nothing Christian about it. It is merely sentimental slush, sloppy shirking of anything that compels national alertness, or effort, or self-discipline, or self-denial; a moral cowardice that pushes away any fact which disturbs a shallow, torpid, irresponsible, self-indulgent optimism.

Our golden age of isolation is over. To attempt to return to it would be a mere pernicious day-dream. To hark back to Washington's warning against entangling alliances is as sensible as to go by a map of the world made in 1796. We are coupled to the company of nations like a car in the middle of a train, only more inevitably and permanently, for we cannot uncouple; and if we tried to do so, we might not wreck the train, but we should assuredly wreck ourselves. I think the war has brought us one benefit certainly: that many young men return from Europe know-

ing this, who had no idea of it before they
went, and who know also that Germany is at
heart an untamed, unchanged wild beast,
never to be trusted again. We must not, and
shall not, boycott her in trade; but let us not
go to sleep at the switch! Just as busily as
she is baking pottery opposite Coblenz, la-
belled "made in St. Louis," "made in Kansas
City," her "army of spies" is at work here
and everywhere to undermine those nations
who have for the moment delayed her plans
for world dominion. I think the number of
Americans who know this has increased; but
no American, wherever he lives, need travel
far from home to meet fellow Americans who
sing the song of slush about forgiving and for-
getting.

Perhaps the man I heard talking in front
of the bulletin board was one of the "army
of spies," as I like to infer from his absence
of "come-back." But perhaps he was merely
an innocent American who at school had
studied, for instance, Eggleston's history;
thoughtless—but by no means harmless; for
his school-taught "slant" against England,
in the days we were living through then,
amounted to a "slant" for Germany. He
would be sorry if Germany beat France, but

not if she beat England—when France and
England were joined in keeping the wolf not
only from their door but from ours! It matters not in the least that they were fighting
our battle, not because they wanted to, but
because they couldn't help it: they were fighting it just the same. That they were compelled doesn't matter, any more than it matters that in going to war when Belgium was
invaded, England's duty and England's self-
interest happened to coincide. Our duty and
our interest also coincided when we entered
the war and joined England and France.
Have we seemed to think that this diminished
our glory? Have they seemed to think that it
absolved them from gratitude?

Such talk as that man's in front of the bulletin board helped Germany then, whether he
meant it to or not, just as much as if a spy
had said it—just as much as similar talk
against England to-day, whether by spies or
unheeding Americans, helps the Germany of
to-morrow. The Germany of yesterday had
her spies all over France and Italy, busily
suggesting to rustic uninformed peasants
that we had gone to France for conquest of
France, and intended to keep some of her
land. What is she telling them now? I don't

know. Something to her advantage and their disadvantage, you may be sure, just as she is busy suggesting to us things to her advantage and our disadvantage—jealousy and fear of the British navy, or pro-German school histories for our children, or that we can't make dyes, or whatever you please: the only sure thing is, that the Germany of yesterday is the Germany of to-morrow. She is not changed. She will not change. The steady stream of her propaganda all over the world proves it. No matter how often her masquerading government changes costumes, that costume is merely her device to conceal the same cunning, treacherous wild beast that in 1914, after forty years of preparation, sprang at the throat of the world. Of all the nations in the late war, she alone is pulling herself together. She is hard at work. She means to spring again just as soon as she can.

Did you read the letter written in April of 1919 by her Vice-Chancellor, Mathias Erzberger, also her minister of finance? A very able, compact masterpiece of malignant voracity, good enough to do credit to Satan. Through that lucky flaw of stupidity which runs through apparently every German brain, and to which we chiefly owe our victory and temporary respite from the fangs of the wolf,

Mathias Erzberger posted his letter. It went wrong in the mails. If you desire to read the whole of it, the International News Bureau can either furnish it or put you on the track of it. One sentence from it shall be quoted here:

"We will undertake the restoration of Russia, and in possession of such support will be ready, within ten or fifteen years, to bring France, without any difficulty, into our power. The march towards Paris will be easier than in 1914. The last step but one towards the world dominion will then be reached. The continent is ours. Afterwards will follow the last stage, the closing struggle, between the continent and the overseas."

Who is meant by "overseas"? Is there left any honest American brain so fond and so feeble as to suppose that we are not included in that highly suggestive and significant term? I fear that some such brains are left.

Germans remain German. I was talking with an American officer just returned from Coblenz. He described the surprise of the Germans when they saw our troops march in to occupy that region of their country. They said to him: "But this is extraordinary. Where do these soldiers of yours come from? You have only 150,000 troops in Europe. All

the other transports were sunk by our submarines." "We have two million troops in
Europe," replied the officer, "and lost by ex-
plosion a very few hundred. No transport
was sunk." "But that is impossible," returned the burgher, "we know from our Government at Berlin that you have only 150,000
troops in Europe."

Germans remain German. At Coblenz they
were servile, cringing, fawning, ready to lick
the boots of the Americans, loading them with
offers of every food and drink and joy they
had. Thus they began. Soon, finding that the
Americans did not cut their throats, burn
their houses, rape their daughters, or bayonet
their babies, but were quiet, civil, disciplined,
and apparently harmless, they changed. Their
fawning faded away, they scowled and mut-
tered. One day the Burgomaster at a certain
place replied to some ordinary requisitions
with an arrogant refusal. It was quite out of
the question, he said, to comply with any such
ridiculous demands. Then the Americans
ceased to seem harmless. Certain steps were
taken by the commanding officer, some leading
citizens   were   collected   and   enlightened
through the only channel whereby light pene-
trates a German skull. Thus, by a very slight
taste of the methods by which they thought

they would cow the rest of the world, these burghers were cowed instantly. They had thought the Americans afraid of them. They had taken civility for fear. Suddenly they encountered what we call the swift kick. It educated them. It always will. Nothing else will.

Mathias Erzberger will, of course, disclaim his letter. He will say it is a forgery. He will point to the protestations of German repentance and reform with which he sweated during April, 1919, and throughout the weeks preceding the delivery of the Treaty at Versailles. Perhaps he has done this already. All Germans will believe him—and some Americans.

The German method, the German madness —what a mixture! The method just grazed making Germany owner of the earth, the madness saved the earth. With perfect recognition of Belgium's share, of Russia's share, of France's, Italy's, England's, our own, in winning the war, I believe that the greatest and most efficient Ally of all who contributed to Germany's defeat was her own constant blundering madness. Americans must never forget either the one or the other, and too many are trying to forget both.

Germans remain German. An American

lady of my acquaintance was about to climb
from Amalfi to Ravello in company with a
German lady of her acquaintance. The German lady had a German Baedeker, the American a Baedeker in English, published several
years apart. The Baedeker in German recommended a path that went straight up the as-
cent, the Baedeker in English a path that
went up more gradually around it. "Mine
says this is the best way," said the American.
"Mine says straight up is the best," said the
German. "But mine is a later edition," said
the American. "That is not it," explained
the German. "It is that we Germans are so
much more clever and agile, that to us is
recommended the more dangerous way while
Americans are shown the safe path."

That happened in 1910. That is *Kultur.*
This too is *Kultur:*

" If Silesia become Polish
Then, oh God, may children perish, like beasts, in their
    mothers' womb.
Then lame their Polish feet and their hands, oh God!
Let them be crippled and blind their eyes.
Smite them with dumbness and madness, both men and
    women."

From a *Hymn of German hate for the Poles.*

Germany remains German; but when next
she springs, she will make no blunders.

V

IT was in Broad Street, Philadelphia, before we went to war, that I overheard the foolish—or propagandist—slur upon England in front of the bulletin board. After we were fighting by England's side for our existence, you might have supposed such talk would cease. It did not. And after the Armistice, it continued. On the day we celebrated as "British Day," a man went through the crowd in Wanamaker's shop, asking, What had England done in the War, anyhow? Was he a German, or an Irishman, or an American in pay of Berlin? I do not know. But this I know: perfectly good Americans still talk like that. Cowboys in camp do it. Men and women in Eastern cities, persons with at least the external trappings of educated intelligence, play into the hands of the Germany of to-morrow, do their unconscious little bit of harm to the future of freedom and civilization, by repeating that England "has always been our enemy." Then they mention the Revolution, the War of 1812, and England's attitude during our Civil War, just as they invariably mentioned these things in 1917 and 1918, when England was our ally in a struggle for life, and as they will be mentioning them in 1940, I presume, if they are still alive at that time.

Now, the Civil War ended fifty-five years ago, the War of 1812 one hundred and five, and the Revolution one hundred and thirty-seven. Suppose, while the Kaiser was butchering Belgium because she barred his way to that dinner he was going to eat in Paris in October, 1914, that France had said, "England is my hereditary enemy. Henry the Fifth and the Duke of Wellington and sundry Plantagenets fought me"; and suppose England had said, "I don't care much for France. Joan of Arc and Napoleon and sundry other French fought me"—suppose they had sat nursing their ancient grudges like that? Well, the Kaiser would have dined in Paris according to his plan. And next, according to his plan, with the Channel ports taken he would have dined in London. And finally, according to his plan, and with the help of his "army of spies" overseas, he would have dined in New York and the White House. For German madness could not have defeated Germany's

plan of World dominion, if various nations
had not got together and assisted. Other
Americans there are, who do not resort to
the Revolution for their grudge, but are in
a commercial rage over this or that: wool,
for instance. Let such Americans reflect that
commercial grievances against England can
be more readily adjusted than an absorption
of all commerce by Germany can be adjusted.
Wool and everything else will belong to Mathias Erzberger and his breed, if they carry
out their intention. And the way to insure
their carrying it out is to let them split us and
England and all their competitors asunder by
their ceaseless and ingenious propaganda,
which plays upon every international prejudice, historic, commercial, or other, which is
available. After August, 1914, England
barred the Kaiser's way to New York, and
in 1917, we found it useful to forget about
George the Third and the *Alabama*. In 1853
Prussia possessed one ship of war—her first.
In 1918 her submarines were prowling along
our coast. For the moment they are no longer
there. For a while they may not be. But do
you think Germany intends that scraps of
paper shall be abolished by any Treaty, even
though it contain 80,000 words and a League

of Nations? She will make of that Treaty a
whole basket of scraps, if she can, and as soon
as she can. She has said so. Her workingmen
are at work, industrious and content with a
quarter the pay for a longer day than any-
where else. Let those persons who cannot get
over George the Third and the *Alabama* ponder upon this for a minute or two.

VI

MUCH else is there that it were well they should ponder, and I am coming to it presently; but first, one suggestion. Most of us, if we dig back only fifty or sixty or seventy years, can disinter various relatives over whose doings we should prefer to glide lightly and in silence.

Do you mean to say that you have none? Nobody stained with any shade of dishonor? No grandfather, great-grandfather, great-great-etc. grandfather or grandmother who ever made a scandal, broke a heart, or betrayed a trust? Every man Jack and woman Jill of the lot right back to Adam and Eve wholly good, honorable, and courageous? How fortunate to be sprung exclusively from the loins of centuries of angels—and to know all about them! Consider the hoard of virtue to which you have fallen heir!

But you know very well that this is not so; that every one of us has every kind of person for an ancestor; that all sorts of virtue and vice, of heroism and disgrace, are mingled in

our blood; that inevitably amidst the huge
herd of our grandsires black sheep as well
as white are to be found.

As it is with men, so it is with nations. Do
you imagine that any nation has a spotless
history? Do you think that you can peer into
our past, turn over the back pages of our record, and never come upon a single blot? Indeed you cannot. And it is better—a great
deal better—that you should be aware of
these blots. Such knowledge may enlighten
you, may make you a better American. What
we need is to be critics of ourselves, and this
is exactly what we have been taught not to be.

We are quite good enough to look straight
at ourselves. Owing to one thing and another
we are cleaner, honester, humaner, and whiter
than any people on the continent of Europe.
If any nation on the continent of Europe has
ever behaved with the generosity and mag-
nanimity that we have shown to Cuba, I have
yet to learn of it. They jeered at us about
Cuba, did the Europeans of the Continent.
Their papers stuck their tongues in their
cheeks. Of course our fine sentiments were
all sham, they said. Of course we intended to
swallow Cuba, and never had intended anything else. And when General Leonard Wood

came away from Cuba, having made Havana healthy, having brought order out of chaos on the island, and we left Cuba independent, Europe jeered on. That dear old Europe!

Again, in 1909, it was not any European nation that returned to China their share of the indemnity exacted in consequence of the Boxer troubles; we alone returned our share to China—sixteen millions. It was we who prevented levying a punitive indemnity on China. Read the whole story; there is much more. We played the gentleman, Europe played the bully. But Europe calls us "dollar chasers." That dear old Europe! Again, if any conquering general on the continent of Europe ever behaved as Grant did to Lee at Appomattox, his name has escaped me.

Again, and lastly—though I am not attempting to tell you here the whole tale of our decencies: Whose hands came away cleanest from that Peace Conference in Paris lately? What did we ask for ourselves? Everything we asked, save some repairs of damage, was for other people. Oh, yes! we are quite good enough to keep quiet about these things. No need whatever to brag. Bragging, moreover, inclines the listener to suspect you're not so remarkable as you sound.

But all this virtue doesn't in the least alter the fact that we're like everybody else in having some dirty pages in our History. These pages it is a foolish mistake to conceal. I suppose that the school histories of every nation are partly bad. I imagine that most of them implant the germ of international hatred in the boys and girls who have to study them. Nations do not like each other, never have liked each other; and it may very well be that school textbooks help this inclination to dislike. Certainly we know what contempt and hatred for other nations the Germans have been sedulously taught in their schools, and how utterly they believed their teaching. How much better and wiser for the whole world if all the boys and girls in all the schools everywhere were henceforth to be started in life with a just and true notion of all flags and the peoples over whom they fly! The League of Nations might not then rest upon the quicksand of distrust and antagonism which it rests upon to-day. But it is our own school histories that are my present concern, and I repeat my opinion—or rather my conviction—that the way in which they have concealed the truth from us is worse than silly, it is harmful. I am not going to take up the whole list of their misrepresentations, I will put but one or two questions to you.

When you finished school, what idea had you about the War of 1812? I will tell you what mine was. I thought we had gone to war because England was stopping American ships and taking American sailors out of them for her own service. I could refer to Perry's victory on Lake Erie and Jackson's smashing of the British at New Orleans; the name of the frigate *Constitution* sent thrills through me. And we had pounded old John Bull and sent him to the right about a second time! Such was my glorious idea, and there it stopped. Did you know much more than that about it when your schooling was done? Did you know that our reasons for declaring war against Great Britain in 1812 were not so strong as they had been three and four years earlier? That during those years England had moderated her arrogance, was ready to moderate further, had placated us for her brutal performance concerning the *Chesapeake,* wanted peace; while we, who had been nearly unanimous for war, and with a fuller purse in 1808, were now, by our own congressional fuddling and messing, without any adequate army, and so divided in

counsel that only one northern state was
wholly in favor of war? Did you know that
our General Hull began by invading Canada
from Detroit and surrendered his whole army
without firing a shot? That the British over-
ran Michigan and parts of Ohio, and western
New York, while we retreated disgracefully?
That though we shone in victories of single
combat on the sea and showed the English
that we too knew how to sail and fight on the
waves as hardily as Britannia (we won eleven
out of thirteen of the frigate and sloop actions), nevertheless she caught us or blocked
us up, and rioted unchecked along our coasts?
You probably did know that the British
burned Washington, and you accordingly
hated them for this barbarous vandalism—
but did you know that we had burned Toronto
a year earlier?

I left school knowing none of this—it
wasn't in my school book, and I learned it in
mature years with amazement. I then learned
also that England, while she was fighting with
us, had her hands full fighting Bonaparte,
that her war with us was a sideshow, and that
this was uncommonly lucky for us—as lucky
quite as those ships from France under Admiral de Grasse, without whose help Washington could never have caught Cornwallis

and compelled his surrender at Yorktown, October 19, 1781. Did you know that there were more French soldiers and sailors than Americans at Yorktown? Is it well to keep these things from the young? I have not done with the War of 1812. There is a political aspect of it that I shall later touch upon—something that my school books never mentioned.

My next question is, what did you know about the Mexican War of 1846–47, when you came out of school? The names of our victories, I presume, and of Zachary Taylor and Winfield Scott; and possibly the treaty of Guadalupe Hidalgo, whereby Mexico ceded to us the whole of Texas, New Mexico, and Upper California, and we paid her fifteen millions. No doubt you know that Santa Anna, the Mexican general, had a wooden leg. Well, there is more to know than that, and I found it out much later. I found out that General Grant, who had fought with credit as a lieutenant in the Mexican War, briefly summarized it as "iniquitous." I gradually, through my reading as a man, learned the truth about the Mexican War which had not been taught me as a boy—that in that war we bullied a weaker power, that we made her our victim, that the whole discreditable business had the extension of slavery at the bottom of it, and that more Americans were against it than had been against the War of 1812. But how many Americans ever learn these things? Do not most of them, upon leaving school, leave history also behind them, and become farmers, or merchants, or plumbers, or firemen, or carpenters, or whatever, and read little but the morning paper for the rest of their lives?

The blackest page in our history would take a long while to read. Not a word of it did I ever see in my school textbooks. They were written on the plan that America could do no wrong. I repeat that, just as we love our friends in spite of their faults, and all the more intelligently because we know these faults, so our love of our country would be just as strong, and far more intelligent, were we honestly and wisely taught in our early years those acts and policies of hers wherein she fell below her lofty and humane ideals. Her character and her record on the whole from the beginning are fine enough to allow the shadows to throw the sunlight into relief. To have produced at three stages of our growth three such men as Washington, Lincoln, and Roosevelt, is quite sufficient justification for our existence.

VII

THE blackest page in our history is our treatment of the Indian. To speak of it is a thankless task—thankless, and necessary.

This land was the Indian's house, not ours. He was here first, nobody knows how many centuries first. We arrived, and we shoved him, and shoved him, and shoved him, back, and back, and back. Treaty after treaty we made with him, and broke. We drew circles round his freedom, smaller and smaller. We allowed him such and such territory, then took it away and gave him less and worse in exchange. Throughout a century our promises to him were a whole basket of scraps of paper. The other day I saw some Indians in California. It had once been their place. All over that region they had hunted and fished and lived according to their desires, enjoying life, liberty, and the pursuit of happiness. We came. To-day the hunting and fishing are restricted by our laws—not the Indian's—because we wasted and almost exterminated in a very short while what had amply provided the Indian with sport and food for a very long while.

In that region we have taken, as usual, the fertile land and the running water, and have allotted land to the Indian where neither wood nor water exist, no crops will grow, no human life can be supported. I have seen the land. I have seen the Indian begging at the back door. Oh, yes, they were an "inferior race." Oh, yes, they didn't and couldn't use the land to the best advantage, couldn't build Broadway and the Union Pacific Railroad, couldn't improve real estate. If you choose to call the whole thing "manifest destiny," I am with you. I'll not dispute that what we have made this continent is of greater service to mankind than the wilderness of the Indian ever could possibly have been—once conceding, as you have to concede, the inevitableness of civilization. Neither you, nor I, nor any man, can remold the sorry scheme of things entire. But we could have behaved better to the Indian. That was in our power. And we gave him a raw deal instead, not once, but again and again. We did it because we could do it without risk, because he was weaker and we could always beat him in the end. And all the while we were doing it, there was our Bill of Rights, our Declaration of Independence, founded on a new thing in the world, proclaiming to mankind the fairest hope yet born, that "All men are endowed by their Creator with certain inalienable rights," and that these were now to be protected by law. Ah, no, look at it as you will, it is a black page, a raw deal. The officers of our frontier army know all about it, because they saw it happen. They saw the treaties broken, the thieving agents, the trespassing settlers, the outrages that goaded the deceived Indian to despair and violence, and when they were ordered out to kill him, they knew that he had struck in self-defense and was the real victim.

It is too late to do much about it now. The good people of the Indian Rights Association try to do something; but in spite of them, what little harm can still be done is being done through dishonest Indian agents and the mean machinery of politics. If you care to know more of the long, bad story, there is a book by Helen Hunt Jackson, *A Century of Dishonor;* it is not new. It assembles and sets forth what had been perpetrated up to the time when it was written. A second volume could be added now.

I have dwelt upon this matter here for a very definite reason, closely connected with my main purpose. It's a favorite trick of our anti-British friends to call England a "land-grabber." The way in which England has grabbed land right along, all over the world, is monstrous, they say. England has stolen what belonged to whites, and blacks, and bronzes, and yellows, wherever she could lay her hands upon it, they say. England is a criminal. They repeat this with great satisfaction, this land-grabbing indictment. Most of them know little or nothing of the facts, couldn't tell you the history of a single case. But what are the facts to the man who asks, "What has England done in this war, anyway?" The word "land-grabber" has been passed to him by German and Sinn Fein propaganda, and he merely parrots it forth. He couldn't discuss it at all. "Look at the Boers," he may know enough to reply, if you remind him that England's land-grabbing was done a good while ago. Well, we shall certainly look at the Boers in due time, but just now we must look at ourselves. I suppose that the American who denounces England for her land-grabbing has forgotten, or else has never known, how we grabbed Florida

from Spain. The pittance that we paid Spain
in one of the Florida transactions never went
to her. The story is a plain tale of land-grabbing; and there are several other plain tales
that show us to have been land-grabbers, if
you will read the facts with an honest mind.
I shall not tell them here. The case of the
Indian is enough in the way of an instance.
Our own hands are by no means clean. It is
not for us to denounce England as a land-
grabber.

You cannot hate statistics more than I do.
But at times there is no dodging them, and
this is one of the times. In 1803 we paid Napoleon Bonaparte fifteen millions for what
was then called Louisiana. Napoleon had his
title to this land from Spain. Spain had it
from France. France had it—how? She had
it because La Salle, a Frenchman, sailed down
the Mississippi River. This gave him title to
the land. There were people on the bank already, long before La Salle came by. It would
have surprised them to be told that the land
was no longer theirs because a man had come
by on the water. But nobody did tell them.
They were Indians. They had wives and children and wigwams and other possessions in
the land where they had always lived; but

they were red, and the man in the boat was white, and therefore they were turned into trespassers because he had sailed by in a boat. That was the title to Louisiana which we bought from Napoleon Bonaparte.

The Louisiana Purchase was a piece of land running up the Mississippi, up the Missouri, over the Divide, and down the Columbia to the Pacific. Before we acquired it, our area was over a quarter, but not half, a million square miles. This added nearly a million square miles more. But what had we really bought? Nothing but stolen goods. The Indians were there before La Salle, from whose boat-sailing the title we bought was derived. "But," you may object, "when whites rob reds or blacks, we call it Discovery; land-grabbing is when whites rob whites—and that is where I blame England." For the sake of argument I concede this, and refer you to our acquisition of Texas. This operation followed some years after the Florida operation. "By request" we "annexed" most of present Texas—in 1845. That was a trick of our slave-holders. They sent people into Texas and these people swung the deal. It was virtually a theft from Mexico. A little while later, in 1848, we "paid" Mexico for Cali-

fornia, Arizona, and Nevada. But if you read
the true story of Frémont in California, and
of the American plots there before the Mexican War, to undermine the government of a
friendly nation, plots connived at in Washington with a view to getting California for
ourselves, upon my word you will find it hard
to talk of England being a land-grabber and
keep a straight face. And, were a certain book
to fall into your hands, the narrative of the
Alcalde of Monterey, wherein he sets down
what of Frémont's doings in California went
on before his eyes, you would learn a story of
treachery, brutality, and greed. All this acquisition of territory, together with the Gads-
den Purchase a few years later, brought our
continent to its present area—not counting
Alaska or some islands later acquired—2,970,-
230 square miles.

Please understand me very clearly: I am
not saying that it has not been far better for
the world and for civilization that we should
have become the rulers of all this land, instead
of its being ruled by the Indians or by Spain,
or by Mexico. That is not at all the point. I
am merely reminding you of the means whereby we got the land. We got it mostly by force
and fraud, by driving out of it through fire-

arms and plots people who certainly were there first and who were weaker than ourselves. Our reason was simply that we wanted it and intended to have it. That is precisely what England has done. She has by various means not one whit better or worse than ours, acquired her possessions in various parts of the world because they were necessary to her safety and welfare, just as this continent was necessary to our safety and welfare. Moreover, the pressure upon her, her necessity for self-preservation, was far more urgent than was the pressure upon us. To make you see this, I must once again resort to some statistics.

England's area—herself and adjacent islands—is 120,832 square miles. Her population in 1811 was eighteen and one half millions. At that same time our area was 408,895 square miles, not counting the recent Louisiana Purchase. And our population was 7,239,881. With an area less than one third of ours (excluding the huge Louisiana) England had a population more than twice as great. Therefore she was more crowded than we were—how much more I leave you to figure out for yourself. I appeal to the fair-minded American reader who only "wants to be shown," and I say to him, when some German or anti-British American talks to him about what a land-grabber England has been in her time, to think of these things and to remember that our own past is tarred with the same stick. Let every one of us bear in mind that little sentence of the Kaiser's, "Even now I rule supreme in the United States"; let us remember that the Armistice and the Peace Treaty do not seem to have altered German nature or German plans very noticeably, and don't let us muddle our brains over the question of the land grabbed by the great-grandfathers of present England.

Any American who is anti-British to-day is by just so much pro-German, is helping the trouble of the world, is keeping discord alight, is doing his bit against human peace and human happiness. There are some other little sentences of the Kaiser and his Huns of which I shall speak before I finish: we must now take up the controversy of those men in front of the bulletin board; we must investigate what lies behind that controversy. Those two men are types. One had learned nothing since he left school, the other had.

VIII

S O far as I know, it was Mr. Sydney George Fisher, an American, who was the first to go back to the original documents, and to write from a study of these documents the complete truth about England and ourselves during the Revolution. His admirable book tore off the cloak which our school histories had wrapped round the facts. He lays bare the political state of Britain at that time. What did you learn at your school of that political state? Did you ever wonder about General Howe and his manner of fighting us? Did it ever strike you that, although we were more often defeated than victorious in those engagements with him (and sometimes he even seemed to avoid pitched battles with us when the odds were all in his favor), yet somehow England didn't seem to reap the advantage she should have reaped from those contests, didn't follow them up, let us get away, didn't in short make any progress to speak of in really conquering us? Perhaps you attributed this to our brave troops and our great Washington. Well, our troops were brave and Washington was great; but there was more behind—more than your school teaching ever led you to suspect, if your schooling was like mine. I imagined England as being just one whole unit of fury and tyranny directed against us and determined to stamp out the spark of liberty we had kindled. No such thing! England was violently divided in sentiment about us. Two parties, almost as opposed as our North and South have been—only it was not sectional in England—held very different views about liberty and the rights of Englishmen. The King's party, George the Third and his upholders, were fighting to saddle autocracy upon England; the other party, that of Pitt and Burke, were resisting this, and their sentiments and political beliefs led them to sympathize with our revolt against George III. "I rejoice," writes Horace Walpole, Dec. 5, 1777, to the Countess of Upper Ossory, "that the Americans are to be free, as they had a right to be, and as I am sure they have shown they deserve to be. . . . I own there are very able Englishmen left, but they happen to be on t'other side of the Atlantic." It was through Whig influence that General

Howe did not follow up his victories over us, because they didn't wish us to be conquered, they wished us to be able to vindicate the rights to which they held all Englishmen were entitled. These men considered us the champions of that British liberty which George III was attempting to crush. They disputed the rightfulness of the Stamp Act. When we refused to submit to the Stamp Tax in 1766, it was then that Pitt exclaimed in Parliament: "I rejoice that America has resisted. . . . If ever this nation should have a tyrant for a King, six millions of freemen, so dead to all the feelings of liberty as voluntarily to submit to be slaves, would be fit instruments to make slaves of the rest." But they were not willing. When the hour struck and the war came, so many Englishmen were on our side that they would not enlist against us, refused to fight us, and George III had to go to Germany and obtain Hessians to help him out. His war against us was lost at home, on English soil, through English disapproval of his course, almost as much as it was lost here through the indomitable Washington and the help of France. That is the actual state of the case, there is the truth. Did you hear much about this at school? Did you ever

learn there that George III had a fake Parliament, largely elected by fake votes, which did
not represent the English people; that this
fake Parliament was autocracy's last ditch in
England; that it choked for a time the English democracy which, after the setback given
it by the excesses of the French Revolution,
went forward again until to-day the King of
England has less power than the President
of the United States? I suppose everybody
in the world who knows the important steps
of history knows this—except the average
American. From him it has been concealed
by his school histories; and generally he
never learns anything about it at all, because
once out of school, he seldom studies any
history again. But why, you may possibly
wonder, have our school histories done this?
I think their various authors may consciously
or unconsciously have felt that our case
against England was not in truth very strong,
that in fact she had been very easy with us,
far easier than any other country was being
with its colonies at that time. The King of
France taxed his colonies, the King of Spain
filled his purse, unhampered, from the pockets
of Mexico and Peru and Cuba and Porto Rico
—from whatever pocket into which he could

put his hand, and the Dutch were doing the same without the slightest question of their right to do it. Our quarrel with the mother country and our breaking away from her in spite of the extremely light rein she was driving us with, rested in reality upon very slender justification. If ever our authors read of the meeting between Franklin, Rutledge, and Adams with General Howe, after the Battle of Long Island, I think they may have felt that we had almost no grievance at all. The plain truth of it was, we had been allowed for so long to be so nearly free that we determined to be free entirely, no matter what England conceded. Therefore these authors of our school textbooks felt that they needed to bolster our cause up for the benefit of the young. Accordingly our boys' and girls' sense of independence and patriotism must be nourished by making England out a far greater oppressor than ever she really had been. These historians dwelt as heavily as they could upon George III and his un-English autocracy, and as lightly as they could upon the English Pitt and upon all the English sympathy we had. Indeed, about this most of them didn't say a word.

Now that policy may possibly have been

desirable once—if it can ever be desirable to suppress historic truth from a whole nation. But to-day, when we have long stood on our own powerful legs and need no bolstering up of such a kind, that policy is not only silly, it is pernicious. It is pernicious because the world is heaving with frightful menaces to all the good that man knows. They would strip life of every resource gathered through centuries of struggle. Mad mobs, whole races of people who have never thought at all, or who have now hurled away all pretense of thought, aim at mere destruction of everything that is. They don't attempt to offer any substitute. Down with religion, down with education, down with marriage, down with law, down with property: Such is their cry. Wipe the slate blank, they say, and then we'll see what we'll write on it. Amid this stands Germany with her unchanged purpose to own the earth; and Japan is doing some thinking. Amid this also is the Anglo-Saxon race, the race that has brought our law, our order, our safety, our freedom into the modern world. That any school histories should hinder the members of this race from understanding each other truly and being friends, should not be tolerated.

Many years later than Mr. Sydney George

Fisher's analysis of England under George III, Mr. Charles Altschul has made an examination and given an analysis of a great number of those school textbooks wherein our boys and girls have been and are still being taught a history of our Revolution in the distorted form that I have briefly summarized. His book was published in 1917 by the George H. Doran Company, New York, and is entitled *The American Revolution in our School Textbooks*. Here following are some of his discoveries:

Of forty school histories used twenty years ago in sixty-eight cities, and in many more unreported, four tell the truth about King George's pocket Parliament, and thirty-two suppress it. To-day our books are not quite so bad, but it is not very much better; and to-day, be it added, any reforming of these textbooks by Boards of Education is likely to be prevented, wherever obstruction is possible, by every influence visible and invisible that pro-German and pro-Irish propaganda can exert. Thousands of our American school children all over our country are still being given a version of our Revolution and the political state of England then, which is as faulty as was George III's government, with its fake parliament, its "rotten boroughs," its Little Sarum. Meanwhile that "army of spies" through which the Kaiser boasted that he ruled "supreme" here, and which, though he is gone, is by no means a demobilized army, but a very busy and well-drilled and well-conducted army, is very glad that our boys and girls should be taught false history, and will do its best to see that they are not taught true history.

Mr. Charles Altschul, in his admirable enterprise, addressed himself to those who preside over our school world all over the country; he received answers from every state in the Union, and he examined ninety-three history textbooks in those passages and pages which they devoted to our Revolution. These books he grouped according to the amount of information they gave about Pitt and Burke and English sympathy with us in our quarrel with George III. These groups are five in number, and dwindle down from group one, "Textbooks which deal fully with the grievances of the colonists, give an account of general political conditions in England prior to the American Revolution, and give credit to prominent Englishmen for the services they rendered the Americans," to

group five, ''Textbooks which deal fully with
the grievances of the colonists, make no reference to general political conditions in England prior to the American Revolution, nor
to any prominent Englishmen who devoted
themselves to the cause of the Americans.''
Of course, what dwindles is the amount said
about our English sympathizers. In groups
three and four this is so scanty as to distort
the truth and send any boy or girl who studied
books of these groups out of school into life
with a very imperfect idea indeed of the size
and importance of English opposition to the
policy of George III; in group five nothing
is said about this at all. The boys and girls
who studied books in group five would grow
up believing that England was undividedly
autocratic, tyrannical, and hostile to our
liberty. In his careful and conscientious
classification, Mr. Altschul gives us the books
in use twenty years ago (and hence responsible for the opinion of Americans now between
thirty and forty years old) and books in use
to-day, and hence responsible for the opinion
of those American men and women who will
presently be grown up and will prolong for
another generation the school-taught ignorance and prejudice of their fathers and

mothers. I select from Mr. Altschul's cata-
logue only those books in use in 1917, when
he published his volume, and of these only
group five, where the facts about English sympathy with us are totally suppressed. *Barnes'
School History of the United States,* by
Steele. *Chandler and Chitword's Makers of
American History. Chambers' (Hansell's) A
School History of the United States. Eggleston's A First Book in American History.
Eggleston's History of the United States and
Its People. Eggleston's New Century History of the United States. Evans' First Les-
sons in Georgia History. Evans' The Essential Facts of American History. Estill's
Beginner's History of Our Country. For-
man's History of the United States. Mont-
gomery's An Elementary American History.
Montgomery's The Beginner's American History. White's Beginner's History of the
United States.*

If the reader has followed me from the
beginning, he will recollect a letter, parts of
which I quoted, from a correspondent who
spoke of Montgomery's history, giving passages in which a fair and adequate recognition of Pitt and our English sympathizers
and their opposition to George III is made.

This would seem to indicate a revision of
the work since Mr. Altschul published his
lists, and to substantiate the hope I expressed
in my original article, and which I here repeat. Surely the publishers of these books
will revise them! Surely any patriotic American publisher and any patriotic board of
education, school principal, or educator, will
watch and resist all propaganda and other
sinister influence tending to perpetuate this
error of these school histories! Whatever
excuse they once had, be it the explanation I
have offered above, or some other, there is
no excuse to-day. These books have laid the
foundation from which has sprung the popular prejudice against England. It has descended from father to son. It has been
further solidified by many tales for boys and
girls, written by men and women who acquired their inaccurate knowledge at our
schools. And it plays straight into the hands
of our enemies.

IX

ALL of these books, history and fiction, drop into the American mind during its early springtime the seed of antagonism, establish in fact an anti-English "complex." It is as pretty a case of complex on the wholesale as could well be found by either historian or psychologist. It is not so violent as the complex which has been planted in the German people by forty years of very adroitly and carefully planned training: they were taught to distrust and hate everybody and to consider themselves so superior to anybody that their sacred duty as they saw it in 1914 was to enslave the world, in order to force upon the world the priceless benefits of their *Kultur*. Under the shock of war that complex dilated into a form of real hysteria or insanity. Our anti-English complex is fortunately milder than that; but none the less does it savor slightly, as any nerve specialist or psychological doctor would tell you —it savors slightly of hysteria, that hundreds of thousands of American men and women

of every grade of education and ignorance
should automatically exclaim whenever the
right button is pressed, "England is a land-
grabber," and "What has England done in
the war?"

The word complex has been in our diction-
ary for a long while. This familiar adjective
has been made by certain scientific people
into a noun, and for brevity and convenience
employed to denote something that almost all
of us harbor in some form or other. These
complexes, these lumps of ideas or impressions that match each other, that are of the
same pattern, and that are also invariably
tinctured with either a pleasurable or painful
emotion, lie buried in our minds, unthought
of but alive, and lurk always ready to set
up a ferment, whenever some new thing from
outside that matches them enters the mind
and hence starts them off. The "suppressed
complex" I need not describe, as our English
complex is by no means suppressed. Known
to us all, probably, is the political complex.
Year after year we have been excited about
elections and candidates and policies, pre-
ferring one party to the other. If this preference has been very marked, or even violent,
you know how disinclined we are to give

credit to the other party for any act or policy,
no matter how excellent in itself, which, had
our own party been its sponsor, we should
have been heart and soul for. You know how
easily we forget the good deeds of the opposite party and how easily we remember its
bad deeds. That's a good simple ordinary
example of a complex. Its workings can be
discerned in the experience of us all. In our
present discussion it is very much to the point.

Established in the soft young minds of our
school boys and girls by a series of reiterated
statements about the tyranny and hostility
of England towards us in the Revolution,
statements which they have to remember and
master by study from day to day, tinctured
by the anxiety about the examination ahead,
when the students must know them or fail,
these incidents of school work being also tinctured by another emotion, that of patriotism,
enthusiasm for Washington, for the Declaration of Independence, for Valley Forge—thus
established in the regular way of all complexes, this anti-English complex is fed and
watered by what we learn of the War of 1812,
by what we learn of the Civil War of 1861,
and by many lesser events in our history thus
far. And just as a Republican will admit

nothing good of a Democrat and a Democrat
nothing good of a Republican because of the
political complex, so does the great—the vast
—majority of Americans automatically and
easily remember everything against England
and forget everything in her favor. Just try
it any day you like. Ask the average American you are sitting next to in a train what
he knows about England; and if he does remember anything and can tell it to you, it
will be unfavorable nine times in ten. The
mere word "England" starts his complex off,
and out comes every fact it has seized that
matches his school-implanted prejudice, just
as it has rejected every fact that does not
match it. There is absolutely no other way to
explain the American habit of speaking ill of
England and well of France. Several times
in the past, France has been flagrantly hostile
to us. But there was Lafayette, there was
Rochambeau, and the great service France
did us then against England. Hence from our
school histories we have a pro-French complex. Under its workings we automatically
remember every good turn France has done
us and automatically forget the evil turns.
Again try the experiment yourself. How
many Americans do you think that you will

find who can recall, or who even know when you recall to them, the insolent and meddlesome Citizen Genet, envoy of the French Republic, and how Washington requested his recall? Or the French privateers that a little later, about 1797–98, preyed upon our commerce? And the hatred of France which many Americans felt and expressed at that time? How many remember that the King of France, directly our Revolution was over, was more hostile to us than England?

X

JACKSTRAWS is a game which most of us have played in our youth. You empty on a table a box of miniature toy rakes, shovels, picks, axes, all sorts of tools and implements. These lie under each other and above each other in intricate confusion, not unlike cross timber in a western forest, only instead of being logs, they are about two inches long and very light. The players sit round the table and with little hooks try in turn to lift one jackstraw out of the heap, without moving any of the others. You go on until you do move one of the others, and this loses you your turn. European diplomacy at any moment of any year reminds you, if you inspect it closely, of a game of jackstraws. Every sort and shape of intrigue is in the general heap and tangle, and the jealous nations sit round, each trying to lift out its own jackstraw. Luckily for us, we have not often been involved in these games of jackstraw hitherto; unlucky for us, we must be henceforth involved. If we kept out, our luck would be still worse.

Immediately after our Revolution, there was one of these heaps of intrigue, in which we were concerned. This was at the time of the negotiations leading to the Treaty of Paris, to which I made reference at the close of the last section. This was in 1783. Twenty years later, in 1803, occurred the heap of jackstraws that led to the Louisiana Purchase. Twenty years later, in 1823, occurred the heap of jackstraws from which emerged the Monroe Doctrine. Each of these dates, dotted along through our early decades, marks a very important crisis in our history. It is well that they should be grouped together, because together they disclose, so to speak, a coherent pattern. This coherent pattern is England's attitude towards ourselves. It is to be perceived, faintly yet distinctly, in 1783, and it grows clearer and ever more clear until in 1898, in the game of jackstraws played when we declared war upon Spain, the pattern is so clear that it could not be mistaken by any one who was not willfully blinded by an anti-English complex. This pattern represents a preference on England's part for ourselves to other nations. I do not ask you to think England's reason for this preference is that she has loved us so much; that she has loved others so much less—there is her reason. She has loved herself better than anybody. So must every nation. So does every nation.

Let me briefly speak of the first game of jackstraws, played at Paris in 1783. Our Revolution was over. The terms of peace had to be drawn. Franklin, Jay, Adams, and Laurens were our negotiators. The various important points were acknowledgment of our independence, settlement of boundaries, freedom of fishing in the neighborhood of the Canadian coast. We had agreed to reach no settlement with England separately from France and Spain. They were our recent friends. England, our recent enemy, sent Richard Oswald as her peace commissioner. This private gentleman had placed his fortune at our disposal during the war, and was Franklin's friend. Lord Shelburne wrote Franklin that if this was not satisfactory, to say so, and name any one he preferred. But Oswald was satisfactory; and David Hartley, another friend of Franklin's and also a sympathizer with our Revolution, was added; and in these circumstances and by these men the

Treaty was made. To France we broke our promise to reach no separate agreement with England. We negotiated directly with the British, and the Articles were signed without consultation with the French Government. When Vergennes, the French Minister, saw the terms, he remarked in disgust that England would seem to have bought a peace rather than made one. By the treaty we got the Northwest Territory and the basin of the Ohio River to the Mississippi. Our recent friend, the French King, was much opposed to our having so much territory. It was our recent enemy, England, who agreed that we should have it. This was the result of that game of jackstraws.

Let us remember several things: in our Revolution, France had befriended us, not because she loved us so much, but because she loved England so little. In the Treaty of Paris, England stood with us, not because she loved us so much, but because she loved France so little. We must cherish no illusions. Every nation must love itself more than it loves its neighbor. Nevertheless, in this pattern of England's policy in 1783, where she takes her stand with us and against other nations, there is a deep significance. Our no-

tions of law, our notions of life, our notions
of religion, our notions of liberty, our notions
of what a man should be and what a woman
should be, are so much more akin to her notions than to those of any other nation, that
they draw her toward us rather than toward
any other nation. That is the lesson of the
first game of jackstraws.

Next comes 1803. Upon the Louisiana Purchase, I have already touched; but not upon
its diplomatic side. In those years the European game of diplomacy was truly porten-
tous. Bonaparte had appeared, and Bonaparte
was the storm centre. From the heap of jackstraws I shall lift out only that which directly
concerns us and our acquisition of that enormous territory, then called Louisiana. Bonaparte had dreamed and planned an empire
over here. Certain vicissitudes disenchanted
him. A plan to invade England also helped
to deflect his mind from establishing an
outpost of his empire upon our continent.
For us he had no love. Our principles were
democratic, he was a colossal autocrat. He
called us "the reign of chatter," and he would
have liked dearly to put out our light. Addington was then the British Prime Minister.
Robert R. Livingston was our minister in

Paris. In the history of Henry Adams, in Volume II at pages 52 and 53, you may find more concerning Bonaparte's dislike of the United States. You may also find that Talleyrand expressed the view that socially and economically England and America were one and indivisible. In Volume I of the same history, at page 439, you will see the mention which Pichon made to Talleyrand of the overtures which England was incessantly making to us. At some time during all this, rumor got abroad of Bonaparte's projects regarding Louisiana. In the second volume of Henry Adams, at pages 23 and 24, you will find Addington remarking to our minister to Great Britain, Rufus King, that it would not do to let Bonaparte establish himself in Louisiana. Addington very plainly hints that Great Britain would back us in any such event. This backing of us by Great Britain found very cordial acceptance in the mind of Thomas Jefferson. A year before the Louisiana Purchase was consummated, and when the threat of Bonaparte was in the air, Thomas Jefferson wrote to Livingston, on April 18, 1802, that "the day France takes possession of New Orleans, we must marry ourselves to the British fleet and nation." In one of his many memoranda to Talleyrand, Livingston alludes to the British fleet. He also points out that France may by taking a certain course estrange the United States for ever and bind it closely to France's great enemy. This particular address to Talleyrand is dated February 1, 1803, and may be found in the Annals of Congress, 1802–1803, at pages 1078 to 1083. I quote a sentence: "The critical moment has arrived which rivets the connexion of the United States to France, or binds a young and growing people for ages hereafter to her mortal and inveterate enemy." After this, hints follow concerning the relative maritime power of France and Great Britain. Livingston suggests that if Great Britain invade Louisiana, who can oppose her? Once more he refers to Great Britain's superior fleet. This interesting address concludes with the following exordium to France: "She will cheaply purchase the esteem of men and the favor of Heaven by the surrender of a distant wilderness, which can neither add to her wealth nor to her strength." This, as you will perceive, is quite a pointed remark. Throughout the Louisiana diplomacy, and negotiations to which this diplomacy led, Livingston's would seem to be the master American mind and prophetic vision. But I must keep to my jackstraws. On April 17, 1803, Bonaparte's brother, Lucien, reports a conversation held with him by Bonaparte. What purposes, what oscillations, may have been going on deep in Bonaparte's secret mind, no one can tell. We may guess that he did not relinquish his plan about Louisiana definitely for some time after the thought had dawned upon him that it would be better if he did relinquish it. But unless he was lying to his brother Lucien on April 17, 1803, we get no mere glimpse, but a perfectly clear sight of what he had come finally to think. It was certainly worth while, he said to Lucien, to sell when you could what you were certain to lose; ''for the English . . . are aching for a chance to capture it. . . . Our navy, so inferior to our neighbor's across the Channel, will always cause our colonies to be exposed to great risks. . . . As to the sea, my dear fellow, you must know that there we have to lower the flag. . . . The English navy is, and long will be, too dominant.''

That was on April 17. On May 2, the Treaty of Cession was signed by the exultant Livingston. Bonaparte, instead of establishing an outpost of autocracy at New Orleans,

sold to us not only the small piece of land
which we had originally in mind, but the huge
piece of land whose dimensions I have given
above. We paid him fifteen millions for
nearly a million square miles. The formal
transfer was made on December 17 of that
same year, 1803. There is my second jackstraw.

Thus, twenty years after the first time in
1783, Great Britain stood between us and the
designs of another nation. To that other nation her fleet was the deciding obstacle. England did not love us so much, but she loved
France so much less. For the same reasons
which I have suggested before, self-interest,
behind which lay her democratic kinship with
our ideals, ranged her with us.

To place my third jackstraw, which follows
twenty years after the second, uninterrupt-
edly in this group, I pass over for the moment
our War of 1812. To that I will return after
I have dealt with the third jackstraw, namely,
the Monroe Doctrine. It was England that
suggested the Monroe Doctrine to us. From
the origin of this in the mind of Canning to
its public announcement upon our side of the
water, the pattern to which I have alluded is
for the third time very clearly to be seen.

How much did your school histories tell you about the Monroe Doctrine? I confess that my notion of it came to this: President Monroe informed the kings of Europe that they must keep away from this hemisphere. Whereupon the kings obeyed him and have remained obedient ever since. Of George Canning I knew nothing. Another large game of jackstraws was being played in Europe in 1823. Certain people there had formed the Holy Alliance. Among these, Prince Metternich the Austrian was undoubtedly the master mind. He saw that by England's victory at Waterloo a threat to all monarchical and dynastic systems of government had been created. He also saw that our steady growth was a part of the same threat. With this in mind, in 1822, he brought about the Holy Alliance. The first Article of the Holy Alliance reads: ''The high contracting Powers, being convinced that the system of representative government is as equally incompatible with the monarchical principle as the maxim of sovereignty of the people with the Divine right, engage mutually, in the most solemn manner, to use all their efforts to put an end to the system of representative governments, in whatever country it may exist in Europe, and to prevent its being introduced in those countries where it is not yet known.''

Behind these words lay a design, hardly veiled, not only against South America, but against ourselves. In a volume entitled *With the Fathers,* by John Bach McMaster, and also in the fifth volume of Mr. McMaster's history, chapter 41, you will find more amply what I abbreviate here. Canning understood the threat to us contained in the Holy Alliance. He made a suggestion to Richard Rush, our minister to England. The suggestion was of such moment, and the ultimate danger to us from the Holy Alliance was of such moment, that Rush made haste to put the matter into the hands of President Monroe. President Monroe likewise found the matter very grave, and he therefore consulted Thomas Jefferson. At that time Jefferson had retired from public life and was living quietly at his place in Virginia. That President Monroe's communication deeply stirred him is to be seen in his reply, written October 24, 1823. Jefferson says in part: ''The question presented by the letters you have sent me is the most momentous which has ever been offered to my contemplation since that of independence. . . . One nation most of all could disturb us. . . . She now offers to lead, aid and accompany us. . . . With her on our side we need not fear the whole world. With her, then, we should most seriously cherish a cordial friendship, and nothing would tend more to unite our affections than to be fighting once more, side by side, in the same cause.''

Thus for the second time, Thomas Jefferson advises a friendship with Great Britain. He realizes as fully as did Bonaparte the power of her navy, and its value to us. It is striking and strange to find Thomas Jefferson, who wrote the Declaration of Independence in 1776, writing in 1823 about uniting our affections and about fighting once more side by side with England.

It was the revolt of the Spanish Colonies from Spain in South America, and Canning's fear that France might obtain dominion in America, which led him to make his suggestion to Rush. The gist of the suggestion was, that we should join with Great Britain in saying that both countries were opposed to any intervention by Europe in the western hemisphere. Over our announcement there was much delight in England. In the London *Courier* occurs a sentence, ''The South American Republics—protected by the two nations that possess the institutions and speak the language of freedom.'' In this fragment from the London *Courier*, the kinship at which I have hinted as being felt by England in 1783, and in 1803, is definitely expressed. From the Holy Alliance, from the general European diplomatic game, and from England's preference for us who spoke her language and thought her thoughts about liberty, law, what a man should be, what a woman should be, issued the Monroe Doctrine. And you will find that no matter what dynastic or ministerial interruptions have occurred to obscure this recognition of kinship with us and preference for us upon the part of the English people, such interruptions are always temporary and lie always upon the surface of English sentiment. Beneath the surface the recognition of kinship persists unchanged and invariably reasserts itself.

That is my third jackstraw. Canning spoke to Rush, Rush consulted Monroe, Monroe consulted Jefferson, and Jefferson wrote what we have seen. That, stripped of every encumbering circumstance, is the story of the Monroe Doctrine. Ever since that day the Monroe Doctrine has rested upon the broad back of the British Navy. This has been no secret to our leading historians, our authoritative writers on diplomacy, and our educated and thinking public men. But they have not generally been eager to mention it; and as to our school textbooks, none that I studied mentioned it at all.

XI

D O not suppose because I am reminding you of these things and shall remind you of some more, that I am trying to make you hate France. I am only trying to persuade you to stop hating England. I wish to show you how much reason you have not to hate her, which your school histories pass lightly over, or pass wholly by. I want to make it plain that your anti-English complex and your pro-French complex entice your memory into retaining only evil about England and only good about France. That is why I pull out from the recorded, certified, and perfectly ascertainable past, these few large facts. They amply justify, as it seems to me, and as I think it must seem to any reader with an open mind, what I said about the pattern.

We must now touch upon the War of 1812. There is a political aspect of this war which casts upon it a light not generally shed by our school histories. Bonaparte is again the point. Nine years after our Louisiana Purchase from him, we declared war upon England. At that moment England was heavily absorbed in her struggle with Bonaparte. It is true that we had a genuine grievance against her. In searching for British sailors upon our ships, she impressed our own. This was our justification.

We made a pretty lame showing, in spite of the victories of our frigates and sloops. Our one signal triumph on land came after the Treaty of Peace had been signed at Ghent. During the years of war, it was lucky for us that England had Bonaparte upon her hands. She could not give us much attention. She was battling with the great Autocrat. We, by declaring war upon her at such a time, played into Bonaparte's hands, and virtually, by embarrassing England, struck a blow on the side of autocracy and against our own political faith. It was a feeble blow, it did but slight harm. And regardless of it England struck Bonaparte down. His hope that we might damage and lessen the power of her fleet that he so much respected and feared, was not realized. We made the Treaty of Ghent. The impressing of sailors from our vessels was tacitly abandoned. The next time that people were removed from vessels, it

was not England who removed them, it was
we ourselves, who had declared war on England for doing so, we ourselves who removed
them from Canadian vessels in the Behring
Sea, and from the British ship *Trent*. These
incidents we shall reach in their proper place.
As a result of the War of 1812, some English
felt justified in taking from us a large slice
of land, but Wellington said, "I think you
have no right, from the state of the war, to
demand any concession of territory from
America." This is all that need be said about
our War of 1812.

Because I am trying to give only the large
incidents, I have intentionally made but a
mere allusion to Florida and our acquisition
of that territory. It was a case again of England's siding with us against a third power,
Spain, in this instance. I have also omitted
any account of our acquisition of Texas, when
England was not friendly—I am not sure
why: probably because of the friction between us over Oregon. But certain other
minor events there are, which do require a
brief reference—the boundaries of Maine, of
Oregon, the Isthmian Canal, Cleveland and
Venezuela, Roosevelt and Alaska; and these
disputes we shall now take up together, be-

fore we deal with the very large matter of our trouble with England during the Civil War. Chronologically, of course, Venezuela and Alaska fall after the Civil War; but they belong to the same class to which Maine and Oregon belong. Together, all of these incidents and controversies form a group in which the underlying permanence of British good-will towards us is distinctly to be discerned. Sometimes, as I have said before, British anger with us obscures the friendly sentiment. But this was on the surface, and it always passed. As usual, it is only the anger that has stuck in our minds. Of the outcome of these controversies and the British temperance and restraint which brought about such outcome the popular mind retains no impression.

The boundary of Maine was found to be undefined to the extent of 12,000 square miles. Both Maine and New Brunswick claimed this, of course. Maine took her coat off to fight, so did New Brunswick. Now, we backed Maine, and voted supplies and men to her. Not so England. More soberly, she said, "Let us arbitrate." We agreed, it was done. By the umpire Maine was awarded more than half what she claimed. And then we disputed the umpire's decision on the ground he hadn't given us the whole thing! Does not this remind you of some of our baseball bad manners? It was settled later, and we got, differently located, about the original award.

Did you learn in school about "fifty-four forty, or fight"? We were ready to take off our coat again. Or at least, that was the platform in 1844 on which President Polk was elected. At that time, what lay between the north line of California and the south line of Alaska, which then belonged to Russia, was called Oregon. We said it was ours. England disputed this. Each nation based its title on discovery. It wasn't really far from an even claim. So Polk was elected, which apparently meant war; his words were bellicose. We blustered rudely. Feeling ran high in England; but she didn't take off her coat. Her ambassador, Pakenham, stiff at first, unbent later. Under sundry missionary impulses, more Americans than British had recently settled along the Columbia River and in the Willamette Valley. People from Missouri followed. You may read of our impatient violence in Professor Dunning's book, *The British Empire and the United States*. Indeed, this volume tells at length everything I am

telling you briefly about these boundary disputes. The settlers wished to be under our
government. Virtually upon their preference
the matter was finally adjusted. England met
us with a compromise, advantageous to us and
reasonable for herself. Thus, again, was her
conduct moderate and pacific. If you think
that this was through fear of us, I can only
leave you to our western blow-hards of 1845,
or to your anti-British complex. What I see
in it, is another sign of that fundamental
sense of kinship, that persisting unwilling-
ness to have a real scrap with us, that stares
plainly out of our whole first century—the
same feeling which prevented so many English from enlisting against us in the Revolution that George III was obliged to get
Hessians.

Nicaragua comes next. There again they
were quite angry with us on top, but con-
trolled in the end by the persisting disposition
of kinship. They had land in Nicaragua with
the idea of an Isthmian Canal. This we did
not like. They thought we should mind our
own business. But they agreed with us in the
Clayton-Bulwer Treaty that both should build
and run the canal. Vagueness about territory
near by raised further trouble, and there we

were in the right. England yielded. The years
went on and we grew, until the time came
when we decided that if there was to be any
canal, no one but ourselves should have it.
We asked to be let off the old treaty. England let us off, stipulating the canal should be
unfortified, and an "open door" to all. Our
representative agreed to this, much to our
displeasure. Indeed, I do not think he should
have agreed to it. Did England hold us to it?
All this happened in the lifetime of many of
us, and we know that she did not hold us to
it. She gave us what we asked, and she did
so because she felt its justice, and that it in
no way menaced her with injury. All this began in 1850 and ended, as we know, in the
time of Roosevelt.

About 1887 our seal-fishing in the Behring
Sea brought on an acute situation. Into the
many and intricate details of this, I need not
go; you can find them in any good encyclope-
dia, and also in *Harper's Magazine* for April,
1891, and in other places. Our fishing clashed
with Canada's. We assumed jurisdiction over
the whole of the sea, which is a third as big as
the Mediterranean, on the quite fantastic
ground that it was an inland sea. Ignoring
the law that nobody has jurisdiction outside

the three-mile limit from their shores, we seized Canadian vessels sixty miles from land. In fact, we did virtually what we had gone to war with England for doing in 1812. But England did not go to war. She asked for arbitration. Throughout this, our tone was raw and indiscreet, while hers was conspicuously the opposite; we had done an unwarrantable and high-handed thing; our claim that Behring Sea was an "inclosed" sea was abandoned; the arbitration went against us, and we paid damages for the Canadian vessels.

In 1895, in the course of a century's dispute over the boundary between Venezuela and British Guiana, Venezuela took prisoner some British subjects, and asked us to protect her from the consequences. Richard Olney, Grover Cleveland's Secretary of State, informed Lord Salisbury, Prime Minister of England, that "in accordance with the Monroe Doctrine, the United States must insist on arbitration"—that is, of the disputed boundary. It was an abrupt extension of the Monroe Doctrine. It was dictating to England the manner in which she should settle a difference with another country. Salisbury declined. On December 17th Cleveland announced to England that the Monroe Doctrine applied to every stage of our national life, and that as Great Britain had for many years refused to submit the dispute to impartial arbitration, nothing remained to us but to accept the situation. Moreover, if the disputed territory was found to belong to Venezuela, it would be the duty of the United States to resist, by every means in its power, the aggressions of Great Britain. This was, in effect, an ultimatum. The stock market went to pieces. In general American opinion, war was coming. The situation was indeed grave. First, we owed the Monroe Doctrine's very existence to English backing. Second, the Doctrine itself had been a declaration against autocracy in the shape of the Holy Alliance, and England was not autocracy. Lastly, as a nation, Venezuela seldom conducted herself or her government on the steady plan of democracy. England was exasperated. And yet England yielded. It took a little time, but arbitration settled it in the end—at about the same time that we flatly declined to arbitrate our quarrel with Spain. History will not acquit us of groundless meddling and arrogance in this matter, while England comes out of it having again shown in the end both forbearance and good manners. Before another Venezuelan incident in 1902, I take up a burning dispute of 1903.

As Oregon had formerly been, so Alaska had later become, a grave source of friction between England and ourselves. Canada claimed boundaries in Alaska which we disputed. This had smouldered along through a number of years until the discovery of gold in the Klondike region fanned it to a somewhat menacing flame. In this instance, history is as unlikely to approve the conduct of the Canadians as to approve our bad manners towards them upon many other occasions. The matter came to a head in Roosevelt's first administration. You will find it all in the *Life of John Hay* by William R. Thayer, Volume II. A commission to settle the matter had dawdled and failed. Roosevelt was tired of delays. Commissioners again were appointed, three Americans, two Canadians, and Alverstone, Lord Chief Justice, to represent England. To his friend Justice Oliver Wendell Holmes, about to sail for an English holiday, Roosevelt wrote a private letter privately to be shown to Mr. Balfour, Mr. Chamberlain, and certain other Englishmen of mark. He said: "The claim of the Canadians for access to deep water along any part of the Alaskan coast is just exactly as indefensible

as if they should now suddenly claim the
Island of Nantucket." Canada had objected
to our Commissioners as being not "impartial
jurists of repute." As to this, Roosevelt's
letter to Holmes ran on: "I believe that no
three men in the United States could be found
who would be more anxious than our own
delegates to do justice to the British claim
on all points where there is even a color of
right on the British side. But the objection
raised by certain British authorities to Lodge,
Root, and Turner, especially to Lodge and
Root, was that they had committed themselves
on the general proposition. No man in public life in any position of prominence could
have possibly avoided committing himself on
the proposition, any more than Mr. Chamberlain could avoid committing himself on the
ownership of the Orkneys if some Scandina-
vian country suddenly claimed them. If this
embodied other points to which there was
legitimate doubt, I believe Mr. Chamberlain
would act fairly and squarely in deciding the
matter; but if he appointed a commission to
settle up all these questions, I certainly
should not expect him to appoint three men,
if he could find them, who believed that as to
the Orkneys the question was an open one. I
wish to make one last effort to bring about an

agreement through the Commission. . . .
But if there is a disagreement . . . I shall
take a position which will prevent any possibility of arbitration hereafter; . . . will render it necessary for Congress to give me the
authority to run the line as we claim it, by
our own people, without any further regard
to the attitude of England and Canada. If I
paid attention to mere abstract rights, that
is the position I ought to take anyhow. I have
not taken it because I wish to exhaust every
effort to have the affair settled peacefully
and with due regard to England's honor.''

That is the way to do these things: not by
a peremptory public letter, like Olney's to
Salisbury, which enrages a whole people and
makes temperate action doubly difficult, but
thus, by a private letter to the proper persons, very plain, very unmistakable, but which
remains private, a sufficient word to the wise,
and not a red rag to the mob. ''To have the
affair settled peacefully and with due regard
to England's honor.'' Thus Roosevelt. England desired no war with us this time, any
more than at the other time. The Commission
went to work, and, after investigating the
facts, decided in our favor.

Our list of boundary episodes finished, I
must touch upon the affair with the Kaiser re-

.

garding Venezuela's debts. She owed money
to Germany, Italy, and England. The Kaiser
got the ear of the Tory government under
Salisbury, and between the three countries a
secret pact was made to repay themselves.
Venezuela is not seldom reluctant to settle
her obligations, and she was slow upon this
occasion. It was the Kaiser's chance—he had
been trying it already at other points—to
slide into a foothold over here under the camouflage of collecting from Venezuela her just
debt to him. So with warships he and his allies established what he called a pacific blockade on Venezuelan ports.

I must skip the comedy that now went on
in Washington (you will find it on pages 287–
288 of Mr. Thayer's *John Hay*, Volume II)
and come at once to Mr. Roosevelt's final
word to the Kaiser, that if there was not an
offer to arbitrate within forty-eight hours,
Admiral Dewey would sail for Venezuela.
In thirty-six hours arbitration was agreed to.
England withdrew from her share in the
secret pact. Had she wanted war with us,
her fleet and the Kaiser's could have out-
matched our own. She did not; and the Kaiser had still very clearly and sorely in remem-
brance what choice she had made between
standing with him and standing with us a few

years before this, upon an occasion that was also connected with Admiral Dewey. This I shall fully consider after summarizing those international episodes of our Civil War wherein England was concerned.

This completes my list of minor troubles with England that we have had since Canning suggested our Monroe Doctrine in 1823. Minor troubles, I call them, because they are all smaller than those during our Civil War. The full record of each is an open page of history for you to read at leisure in any good library. You will find that the anti-English complex has its influence sometimes in the pages of our historians, but Professor Dunning is free from it. You will find, whatever transitory gusts of anger, jealousy, hostility, or petulance may have swept over the English people in their relations with us, these gusts end in a calm; and this calm is due to the common-sense of the race. It revealed itself in the treaty at the close of our Revolution, and it has been the ultimate controlling factor in English dealings with us ever since. And now I reach the last of my large historic matters, the Civil War, and our war with Spain.

XII

ON THE RAGGED EDGE

ON November 6, 1860, Lincoln, nominee of the Republican party, which was opposed to the extension of slavery, was elected President of the United States. Forty-one days later, the legislature of South Carolina, determined to perpetuate slavery, met at Columbia, but, on account of a local epidemic, moved to Charleston. There, about noon, December 20th, it unanimously declared "that the Union now subsisting between South Carolina and other States, under the name of the United States of America, is hereby dissolved." Soon other slave states followed this lead, and among them all, during those final months of Buchanan's presidency, preparedness went on, unchecked by the half-feeble, half-treacherous Federal Government. Lincoln, in his inaugural address, March 4, 1861, declared that he had no purpose, directly or indirectly, to interfere with the institution of slavery in the states where it existed. To the seceded slave states he said: "In your hands, my dissatisfied fellow-countrymen, and not mine, is the momentous issue of civil war. The Government will not assail you. You can have no conflict without being yourselves the aggressors. You can have no oath registered in heaven to destroy the Government; while I shall have the most solemn one to preserve, protect and defend it." This changed nothing in the slave states. It was not enough for them that slavery could keep on where it was. To spread it where it was not, had been their aim for a very long while. The next day, March 5th, Lincoln had letters from Fort Sumter, in Charleston harbor. Major Anderson was besieged there by the batteries of secession, was being starved out, might hold on a month longer, needed help. Through staggering complications and embarrassments, which were presently to be outstaggered by worse ones, Lincoln by the end of March saw his path clear. "In your hands, my dissatisfied fellow-countrymen, and not mine, is the momentous issue of civil war." The clew to the path had been in those words from the first. The flag of the Union, the little island of loyalty amid the waters of secession, was covered by the Charleston batteries. "Batteries ready to open Wednesday or Thursday. What instructions?" Thus, on

April 1st, General Beauregard, at Charleston, telegraphed to Jefferson Davis. They had all been hoping that Lincoln would give Fort Sumter to them and so save their having to take it. Not at all. The President of the United States was not going to give away property of the United States. Instead, the Governor of South Carolina received a polite message that an attempt would be made to supply Fort Sumter with food only, and that if this were not interfered with, no arms or ammunition should be sent there without further notice, or in case the fort were attacked. Lincoln was leaning backwards, you might say, in his patient effort to conciliate. And accordingly our transports sailed from New York for Charleston with instructions to supply Sumter with food alone, unless they should be opposed in attempting to carry out their errand. This did not suit Jefferson Davis at all; and, to cut it short, at half-past four, on the morning of April 12, 1861, there arose into the air from the mortar battery near old Fort Johnson, on the south side of the harbor, a bomb-shell, which curved high and slow through the dawn, and fell upon Fort Sumter, thus starting four years of civil war. One week later the Union proclaimed a blockade on the ports of Slave Land.

Bear each and all of these facts in mind, I beg, bear them in mind well, for in the light of them you can see England clearly, and will have no trouble in following the different threads of her conduct towards us during this struggle. What she did then gave to our ancient grudge against her the reddest coat of fresh paint which it had received yet—the reddest and the most enduring since George III.

England ran true to form. It is very interesting to mark this; very interesting to watch in her government and her people the persistent and conflicting currents of sympathy and antipathy boil up again, just as they had boiled in 1776. It is equally interesting to watch our ancient grudge at work, causing us to remember and hug all the ill will she bore us, all the harm she did us, and to forget all the good. Roughly comparing 1776 with 1861, it was once more the Tories, the aristocrats, the Lord Norths, who hoped for our overthrow, while the people of England, with certain liberal leaders in Parliament, stood our friends. Just as Pitt and Burke had spoken for us in our Revolution, so Bright and Cobden befriended us now. The parallel ceases

when you come to the Sovereign. Queen Victoria declined to support or recognize Slave
Land. She stopped the Government and aristocratic England from forcing war upon us,
she prevented the French Emperor, Napoleon
III, from recognizing the Southern Confederacy. We shall come to this in its turn. Our
Civil War set up in England a huge vibration,
subjected England to a searching test of herself. Nothing describes this better than a letter of Henry Ward Beecher's, written during
the War, after his return from addressing the
people of England.

"My own feelings and judgment underwent
a great change while I was in England . . . I
was chilled and shocked at the coldness
towards the North which I everywhere met,
and the sympathetic prejudices in favor of the
South. And yet everybody was alike con-
demning slavery and praising liberty!"

How could England do this, how with the
same breath blow cold and hot, how be against
the North that was fighting the extension of
slavery and yet be against slavery too? Con-
fusing at the time, it is clear to-day. Im-
bedded in Lincoln's first inaugural address
lies the clew: he said, "I have no purpose,
directly or indirectly, to interfere with the

institution of slavery where it exists. I believe I have no lawful right to do so, and I
have no inclination to do so. Those who
elected me did so with full knowledge that I
had made this and many similar declarations,
and had never recanted them." Thus Lincoln, March 4, 1861. Six weeks later, when
we went to war, we went, not "to interfere
with the institution of slavery," but (again
in Lincoln's words) "to preserve, protect,
and defend" the Union. This was our slogan,
this our fight, this was repeated again and
again by our soldiers and civilians, by our
public men and our private citizens. Can you
see the position of those Englishmen who con-
demned slavery and praised liberty? We ourselves said we were not out to abolish slavery,
we disclaimed any such object, by our own
words we cut the ground away from them.
Not until September 22d of 1862, to take effect upon January 1, 1863, did Lincoln pro-
claim emancipation—thus doing what he had
said twenty-two months before "I believe I
have no lawful right to do."

That interim of anguish and meditation had
cleared his sight. Slowly he had felt his way,
slowly he had come to perceive that the preservation of the Union and the abolition of

slavery were so tightly wrapped together as to merge and be one and the same thing. But even had he known this from the start, known that the North's bottom cause, the ending of slavery, rested on moral ground, and that moral ground outweighs and must forever outweigh whatever of legal argument may be on the other side, he could have done nothing. "I believe I have no lawful right." There were thousands in the North who also thus believed. It was only an extremist minority who disregarded the Constitution's acquiescence in slavery and wanted emancipation proclaimed at once. Had Lincoln proclaimed it, the North would have split in pieces, the South would have won, the Union would have perished, and slavery would have remained. Lincoln had to wait until the season of anguish and meditation had unblinded thousands besides himself, and thus had placed behind him enough of the North to struggle on to that saving of the Union and that freeing of the slave which was consummated more than two years later by Lee's surrender to Grant at Appomattox.

But it was during that interim of anguish and meditation that England did us most of the harm which our memories vaguely but violently treasure. Until the Emancipation, we gave our English friends no public, official grounds for their sympathy, and consequently their influence over our English enemies was hampered. Instantly after January 1, 1863, that sympathy became the deciding voice. Our enemies could no longer say to it, "but Lincoln says himself that he doesn't intend to abolish slavery."

Here are examples of what occurred: To William Lloyd Garrison, the Abolitionist, an English sympathizer wrote that three thousand men of Manchester had met there and adopted by acclamation an enthusiastic message to Lincoln. These men said that they would rather remain unemployed for twenty years than get cotton from the South at the expense of the slave. A month later Cobden writes to Charles Sumner: "I know nothing in my political experience so striking, as a display of spontaneous public action, as that of the vast gathering at Exeter Hall (in London), when, without one attraction in the form of a popular orator, the vast building, its minor rooms and passages, and the streets adjoining, were crowded with an enthusiastic audience. That meeting has had a powerful effect on our newspapers and politicians. It has closed the mouths of those who have been advocating the side of the South. And I now write to assure you that any unfriendly act on the part of our Government—no matter which of our aristocratic parties is in power —towards your cause is not to be apprehended. If an attempt were made by the Government in any way to commit us to the South, a spirit would be instantly aroused which would drive that Government from power."

I lay emphasis at this point upon these instances (many more could be given) because it has been the habit of most Americans to say that England stopped being hostile to the North as soon as the North began to win. In January, 1863, the North had not visibly begun to win, it had suffered almost unvaried defeat so far; and the battles of Gettysburg and Vicksburg, where the tide turned at last our way, were still six months ahead. It was from January 1, 1863, when Lincoln planted our cause firmly and openly on abolition ground, that the undercurrent of British sympathy surged to the top. The true wonder is, that this undercurrent should have been so strong all along, that those English sympathizers somehow in their hearts should have known what we were fighting for more clearly than we had been able to see it ourselves. The key to this is given in Beecher's letter—it is nowhere better given—and to it I must now return.

"I soon perceived that my first error was in supposing that Great Britain was an impartial spectator. In fact, she was morally an actor in the conflict. Such were the antagonistic influences at work in her own midst, and the division of parties, that, in judging American affairs she could not help lending sanction to one or the other side of her own internal conflicts. England was not, then, a judge, sitting calmly on the bench to decide without bias; the case brought before her was her own, in principle, and in interest. In taking sides with the North, the common people of Great Britain and the laboring class took sides with themselves in their struggle for reformation; while the wealthy and the privileged classes found a reason in their own political parties and philosophies why they should not be too eager for the legitimate government and nation of the United States.

"All classes who, at home, were seeking the elevation and political enfranchisement of the common people were with us. All who studied the preservation of the state in its present unequal distribution of political privileges, sided with that section in America that were doing the same thing.

"We ought not to be surprised nor angry that men should maintain aristocratic doctrines which they believe in fully as sincerely, and more consistently, than we, or many amongst us do, in democratic doctrines.

"We of all people ought to understand how a government can be cold or semi-hostile, while the people are friendly with us. For thirty years the American Government, in the hands, or under the influence of Southern statesmen, has been in a threatening attitude to Europe, and actually in disgraceful conflict with all the weak neighboring Powers. Texas, Mexico, Central America, and Cuba are witnesses. Yet the great body of our people in the Middle and Northern States are strongly opposed to all such tendencies."

It was in a very brief visit that Beecher managed to see England as she was: a remarkable letter for its insight, and more remarkable still for its moderation, when you consider that it was written in the midst of our Civil War, while loyal Americans were not only enraged with England, but wounded to the quick as well. When a man can do this —can have passionate convictions in passionate times, and yet keep his judgment unclouded, wise, and calm, he serves his country well.

I can remember the rage and the wound. In that atmosphere I began my existence. My childhood was steeped in it. In our house the London *Punch* was stopped, because of its hostile ridicule. I grew to boyhood hearing from my elders how England had for years taunted us with our tolerance of slavery while we boasted of being the Land of the Free— and then, when we arose to abolish slavery, how she "jack-knived" and gave aid and comfort to the slave power when it had its fingers upon our throat. Many of that generation of my elders never wholly got over the rage and the wound. They hated all England for the sake of less than half England. They counted their enemies but never their friends. There's nothing unnatural about this, nothing rare. On the contrary, it's the usual, natural, unjust thing that human nature does in times of agony. It's the Henry Ward Beechers that are rare. In times of agony the average man and woman see nothing but their agony. When I look over some of the letters that I re-

ceived from England in 1915—letters from
strangers evoked by a book called *The Pentecost of Calamity,* wherein I had published my
conviction that the cause of England was
righteous, the cause of Germany hideous, and
our own persistent neutrality unworthy—I'm
glad I lost my temper only once, and replied
caustically only once. How dreadful (wrote
one of my correspondents) must it be to belong to a nation that was behaving like mine!
I retorted (I'm sorry for it now) that I
could all the more readily comprehend English feeling about our neutrality, because I
had known what we had felt when Gladstone
spoke at Newcastle and when England let the
Alabama loose upon us in 1862. Where was
the good in replying at all? Silence is almost
always the best reply in these cases. Next
came a letter from another English stranger,
in which the writer announced having just
read *The Pentecost of Calamity.* Not a word
of friendliness for what I had said about the
righteousness of England's cause or my expressed unhappiness over the course which
our Government had taken—nothing but
scorn for us all and the hope that we should
reap our deserts when Germany defeated
England and invaded us. Well? What of it?

Here was a stricken person, writing in stress, in a land of desolation, mourning for the dead already, waiting for the next who should die, a poor, unstrung average person, who had not long before read that remark of our President's made on the morrow of the *Lusitania:* that there is such a thing as being too proud to fight; had read during the ensuing weeks those notes wherein we stood committed by our Chief Magistrate to a verbal slinking away and sitting down under it. Can you wonder? If the mere memory of those days of our humiliation stabs me even now, I need no one to tell me (though I have been told) what England, what France, felt about us then, what it must have been like for Americans who were in England and France at that time. No: the average person in great trouble cannot rise above the trouble and survey the truth and be just. In English eyes our Government—and therefore all of us—failed in 1914—1915—1916—failed again and again— insulted the cause of humanity when we said through our President in 1916, the *third* summer of the war, that we were not concerned with either the causes or the aims of that conflict. How could they remember Hoover, or Robert Bacon, or Leonard Wood, or Theo-

dore Roosevelt then, any more than we could
remember John Bright, or Richard Cobden,
or the Manchester men in the days when the
Alabama was sinking the merchant vessels of
the Union?

We remembered Lord John Russell and
Lord Palmerston in the British Government,
and their fellow aristocrats in British society;
we remembered the aristocratic British press
—*The Times* notably, because the most powerful—these are what we saw, felt, and remembered, because they were not with us, and
were able to hurt us in the days when our
friends were not yet able to help us. They
made welcome the Southerners who came over
in the interests of the South, they listened to
the Southern propaganda. Why? Because
the South was the American version of their
aristocratic creed. To those who came over
in the interests of the North and of the Union
they turned a cold shoulder, because they represented Democracy; moreover, a Dis-United
States would prove in commerce a less formidable competitor. To Captain Bullock, the
able and energetic Southerner who put
through in England the building and launch-
ing of those Confederate cruisers which sank
our ships and destroyed our merchant ma-

rine, and to Mason and Slidell, the doors of dukes opened pleasantly; Beecher and our other emissaries mostly had to dine beneath uncoroneted roofs.

In the pages of Henry Adams, and of Charles Francis Adams his brother, you can read of what they, as young men, encountered in London, and what they saw their father have to put up with there, both from English society and the English Government. Their father was our new minister to England, appointed by Lincoln. He arrived just after our Civil War had begun. I have heard his sons talk about it familiarly, and it is all to be found in their writings.

Nobody knows how to be disagreeable quite so well as the English gentleman, except the English lady. They can do it with the nicety of a medicine dropper. They can administer the precise *quantum suff.* in every case. In the society of English gentlemen and ladies Mr. Adams by his official position was obliged to move. They left him out as much as they could, but, being the American Minister, he couldn't be left out altogether. At their dinners and functions he had to hear open expressions of joy at the news of Southern victories, he had to receive slights both veiled

and unveiled, and all this he had to bear with
equanimity. Sometimes he did leave the
room; but with dignity and discretion. A
false step, a "break," might have led to a request for his recall. He knew that his constant presence, close to the English Government, was vital to our cause. Russell and
Palmerston were by turns insolent and shifty,
and once on the very brink of recognizing the
Southern Confederacy as an independent nation. Gladstone, Chancellor of the Exchequer,
in a speech at Newcastle, virtually did recognize it. You will be proud of Mr. Adams if
you read how he bore himself and fulfilled his
appallingly delicate and difficult mission. He
was an American who knew how to behave
himself, and he behaved himself all the time;
while the English had a way of turning their
behavior on and off, like the hot water. Mr.
Adams was no admirer of "shirt-sleeves"
diplomacy. His diplomacy wore a coat. Our
experiments in "shirt-sleeves" diplomacy
fail to show that it accomplishes anything
which diplomacy decently dressed would not
accomplish more satisfactorily. Upon Mr.
Adams fell some consequences of previous
American crudities, of which I shall speak
later.

Lincoln had declared a blockade on Southern ports before Mr. Adams arrived in London. Upon his arrival he found England had proclaimed her neutrality and recognized the belligerency of the South. This dismayed Mr. Adams and excited the whole North, because feeling ran too high to perceive this first act on England's part to be really favorable to us; she could not recognize our blockade, which stopped her getting Southern cotton, unless she recognized that the South was in a state of war with us. Looked at quietly, this act of England's helped us and hurt herself, for it deprived her of cotton.

It was not with this, but with the reception and treatment of Mr. Adams that the true hostility began. Slights to him were slaps at us, sympathy with the South was an active moral injury to our cause, even if it was mostly an undertone, politically. Then all of a sudden, something that we did ourselves changed the undertone to a loud overtone, and we just grazed England's declaring war on us. Had she done so, then indeed it had been all up with us. This incident is the comic going-back on our own doctrine of 1812, to which I have alluded above.

On November 8, 1861, Captain Charles

Wilkes of the American steam-sloop *San Ja-cinto*, fired a shot across the bow of the British vessel *Trent*, stopped her on the high seas, and took four passengers off her, and brought them prisoners to Fort Warren, in Boston harbor. Mason and Slidell are the two we remember, Confederate envoys to France and Great Britain. Over this the whole North burst into glorious joy. Our Secretary of the Navy wrote to Wilkes his congratulations, Congress voted its thanks to him, governors and judges laureled him with oratory at banquets, he was feasted with meat and drink all over the place, and, though his years were sixty-three, ardent females probably rushed forth from throngs and kissed him with the purest intentions: heroes have no age. But presently the *Trent* arrived in England, and the British lion was aroused. We had violated international law, and insulted the British flag. Palmerston wrote us a letter—or Russell, I forget which wrote it—a letter that would have left us no choice but to fight. But Queen Victoria had to sign it before it went. "My lord," she said, "you must know that I will agree to no paper that means war with the United States." So this didn't go, but another in its stead, pretty stiff, naturally,

yet still possible for us to swallow. Some
didn't want to swallow even this; but Lincoln,
humorous and wise, said, "Gentlemen, one
war at a time"; and so we made due restitu-
tion, and Messrs. Mason and Slidell went
their way to France and England, free to
bring about action against us there if they
could manage it. Captain Wilkes must have
been a good fellow. His picture suggests this.
England, in her English heart, really liked
what he had done, it was in its gallant fla-
grancy so remarkably like her own doings—
though she couldn't naturally, permit such
a performance to pass; and a few years afterwards, for his services in the cause of ex-
ploration, her Royal Geographical Society
gave him a gold medal! Yes; the whole thing
is comic—to-day; for us, to-day, the point of
it is, that the English queen saved us from a
war with England.

Within a year, something happened that
was not comic. Lord John Russell, though
warned and warned, let the *Alabama* slip
away to sea, where she proceeded to send our
merchant ships to the bottom, until the *Kear-
sarge* sent her herself to the bottom. She had
been built at Liverpool in the face of an English law which no quibbling could disguise to

anybody except to Lord John Russell and to those who, like him, leaned to the South. Ten years later, this leaning cost England fifteen million dollars in damages.

Let us now listen to what our British friends were saying in those years before Lincoln issued his Emancipation Proclamation. His blockade had brought immediate and heavy distress upon many English workmen and their families. That had been April 19, 1861. By September, five sixths of the Lancashire cotton-spinners were out of work, or working half time. Their starvation and that of their wives and children could be stemmed by charity alone. I have talked with people who saw those thousands in their suffering. Yet those thousands bore it. They somehow looked through Lincoln's express disavowal of any intention to interfere with slavery, and saw that at bottom our war was indeed against slavery, that slavery was behind the Southern camouflage about independence, and behind the Northern slogan about preserving the Union. They saw and they stuck. "Rarely," writes Charles Francis Adams, "in the history of mankind, has there been a more creditable exhibition of human sympathy." France was likewise damaged by

our blockade; and Napoleon III would have
liked to recognize the South. He established,
through Maximilian, an empire in Mexico, behind which lay hostility to our Democracy.
He wished us defeat; but he was afraid to
move without England, to whom he made
a succession of indirect approaches. These
nearly came to something towards the close
of 1862. It was on October 7th that Gladstone
spoke at Newcastle about Jefferson Davis
having made a nation. Yet, after all, England
didn't budge, and thus held Napoleon back.
From France in the end the South got neither
ships nor recognition, in spite of his deceitful
connivance and desire; Napoleon flirted a
while with Slidell, but grew cold when he saw
no chance of English co-operation.

Besides John Bright and Cobden, we had
other English friends of influence and celeb-
rity: John Stuart Mill, Thomas Hughes,
Goldwin Smith, Leslie Stephen, Robert Gladstone, Frederic Harrison are some of them.
All from the first supported us. All from the
first worked and spoke for us. The Union and
Emancipation Society was founded. "Your
Committee," says its final report when the
war was ended, "have issued and circulated
upwards of four hundred thousand books,

pamphlets, and tracts . . . and nearly five
hundred official and public meetings have been
held. . . ." The president of this Society, Mr.
Potter, spent thirty thousand dollars in the
cause, and at a time when times were hard and
fortunes as well as cotton-spinners in distress
through our blockade. Another member of
the Society, Mr. Thompson, writes of one of
the public meetings: ". . . I addressed a
crowded assembly of unemployed operatives
in the town of Heywood, near Manchester,
and spoke to them for two hours about the
Slaveholders' Rebellion. They were united
and vociferous in the expression of their
willingness to suffer all hardships consequent
upon a want of cotton, if thereby the liberty
of the victims of Southern despotism might
be promoted. All honor to the half million of
our working population in Lancashire, Chesh-
ire, and elsewhere, who are bearing with heroic fortitude the privation which your war
has entailed upon them! . . . Their sublime
resignation, their self-forgetfulness, their observance of law, their whole-souled love of
the cause of human freedom, their quick and
clear perception of the merits of the question
between the North and the South . . . are ex-
torting the admiration of all classes of the
community. . . ."

How much of all this do you ever hear from the people who remember the *Alabama?*

Strictly in accord with Beecher's vivid summary of the true England in our Civil War, are some passages of a letter from Mr. John Bigelow, who was at that time our Consul-General at Paris, and whose impressions, written to our Secretary of State, Mr. Seward, on February 6, 1863, are interesting to compare with what Beecher says in that letter, from which I have already given extracts.

"The anti-slavery meetings in England are having their effect upon the Government already. . . . The Paris correspondent of the *London Post* also came to my house on Wednesday evening. . . . He says . . . that there are about a dozen persons who by their position and influence over the organs of public opinion have produced all the bad feeling and treacherous conduct of England towards America. They are people who, as members of the Government in times past, have been bullied by the U. S. . . . they are not entirely ignorant that the class who are now trying to overthrow the Government were mainly responsible for the brutality, but they think we as a nation are disposed to bully, and they are disposed to assist in any policy that may dismember and weaken us. These scars of

wounded pride, however, have been carefully
concealed from the public, who therefore cannot be readily made to see why, when the
President has distinctly made the issue between slave labor and free labor, that England should not go with the North. He says
these dozen people who rule England hate us
cordially. . . .''

There were more than a dozen, a good many
more, as we know from Charles and Henry
Adams. But read once again the last para-
graph of Beecher's letter, and note how it
corresponds with what Mr. Bigelow says
about the feeling which our Government (for
thirty years ''in the hands or under the influence of Southern statesmen'') had raised
against us by its bad manners to European
governments. This was the harvest sown by
shirt-sleeves diplomacy and reaped by Mr.
Adams in 1861. Only seven years before, we
had gratuitously offended four countries at
once. Three of our foreign ministers (two of
them from the South) had met at Ostend and
later at Aix in the interests of extending slavery, and there, in a joint manifesto, had ordered Spain to sell us Cuba, or we would take
Cuba by force. One of the three was our minister to Spain. Spain had received him cour-

teously as the representative of a nation with whom she was at peace. It was like ringing the doorbell of an acquaintance, being shown into the parlor and telling him he must sell you his spoons or you would snatch them. This doesn't incline your neighbor to like you. But, as has been said, Mr. Adams was an American who did know how to behave, and thereby served us well in our hour of need.

We remember the *Alabama* and our English enemies, we forget Bright, and Cobden, and all our English friends; but Lincoln did not forget them. When a young man, a friend of Bright's, an Englishman, had been caught here in a plot to seize a vessel and make her into another *Alabama,* John Bright asked mercy for him; and here are Lincoln's words in consequence:

"Whereas one Rubery was convicted on or about the twelfth day of October, 1863, in the Circuit Court of the United States for the District of California, of engaging in, and giving aid and comfort to the existing rebellion against the Government of this Country, and sentenced to ten years' imprisonment, and to pay a fine of ten thousand dollars;

"And whereas, the said Alfred Rubery is

of the immature age of twenty years, and of
highly respectable parentage;

"And whereas, the said Alfred Rubery is
a subject of Great Britain, and his pardon is
desired by John Bright, of England;

"Now, therefore, be it known that I, Abra-
ham Lincoln, President of the United States
of America, these and divers other considerations me thereunto moving, and especially as
a public mark of the esteem held by the
United States of America for the high character and steady friendship of the said John
Bright, do hereby grant a pardon to the said
Alfred Rubery, the same to begin and take
effect on the twentieth day of January, 1864,
on condition that he leave the country within
thirty days from and after that date."

Thus Lincoln, because of Bright; and because of a word from Bright to Charles Sumner about the starving cotton-spinners, Americans sent from New York three ships with
flour for those faithful English friends of
ours.

And then, at Geneva in 1872, England paid
us for what the *Alabama* had done. This
Court of Arbitration grew slowly; suggested
first by Mr. Thomas Balch to Lincoln, who
thought the millennium wasn't quite at hand

but favored "airing the idea." The idea was not aired easily. Cobden would have brought it up in Parliament, but illness and death overtook him. The idea found but few other friends. At last Horace Greeley "aired" it in his paper. On October 23, 1863, Mr. Adams said to Lord John Russell, "I am directed to say that there is no fair and equitable form of conventional arbitrament or reference to which the United States will not be willing to submit." This, some two years later, Russell recalled, saying in reply to a statement of our grievances by Adams: "It appears to Her Majesty's Government that there are but two questions by which the claim of compensation could be tested; the one is, Have the British Government acted with due diligence, or, in other words, in good faith and honesty, in the maintenance of the neutrality they proclaimed? The other is, Have the law officers of the Crown properly understood the foreign enlistment act, when they declined, in June 1862, to advise the detention and seizure of the *Alabama,* and on other occasions when they were asked to detain other ships, building or fitting in British ports? It appears to Her Majesty's Government that neither of these questions could

be put to a foreign government with any regard to the dignity and character of the
British Crown and the British Nation. Her
Majesty's Government are the sole guardians
of their own honor. They cannot admit that
they have acted with bad faith in maintaining
the neutrality they professed. The law officers
of the Crown must be held to be better in-
terpreters of a British statute than any
foreign Government can be presumed to be.
. . ." He consented to a commission, but
drew the line at any probing of England's
good faith.

We persisted. In 1868, Lord Westbury,
Lord High Chancellor, declared in the House
of Lords that "the animus with which the
neutral powers acted was the only true
criterion."

This is the test which we asked should be
applied. We quoted British remarks about
us, Gladstone, for example, as evidence of
unfriendly and insincere animus on the part
of those at the head of the British Government.

Replying to our pressing the point of
animus, the British Government reasserted
Russell's refusal to recognize or entertain
any question of England's good faith: "first,

because it would be inconsistent with the self-respect which every government is bound to feel. . . ." In Mr. John Bassett Moore's *History of International Arbitration,* Vol. I, pages 496–497, or in papers relating to the Treaty of Washington, Vol. II, *Geneva Arbitration,* page 204 . . . Part 1, Introductory Statement, you will find the whole of this. What I give here suffices to show the position we ourselves and England took about the *Alabama* case. She backed down. Her good faith was put in issue, and she paid our direct claims. She ate "humble pie." We had to eat humble pie in the affair of the *Trent.* It has been done since. It is not pleasant, but it may be beneficial.

Such is the story of the true England and the true America in 1861; the divided North with which Lincoln had to deal, the divided England where our many friends could do little to check our influential enemies, until Lincoln came out plainly against slavery. I have had to compress much, but I have omitted nothing material, of which I am aware. The facts would embarrass those who determine to assert that England was our undivided enemy during our Civil War, if facts ever embarrassed a complex. Those

afflicted with the complex can keep their eyes
upon the *Alabama* and the London *Times,* and
avert them from Bright, and Cobden, and the
cotton-spinners, and the Union and Emancipation Society, and Queen Victoria. But to
any reader of this whose complex is not in-
curable, or who has none, I will put this question: What opinion of the brains of any Englishman would you have if he formed his
idea of the United States exclusively from the
newspapers of William Randolph Hearst?

XIII

BENEFITS FORGOT

IN our next war, our war with Spain in 1898,
England saved us from Germany. She did
it from first to last; her position was unmistakable, and every determining act of hers
was as our friend. The service that she
rendered us in warning Germany to keep out
of it, was even greater than her suggestion of
our Monroe Doctrine in 1823; for in 1823 she
put us on guard against meditated, but remote, assault from Europe, while in 1898 she
actively averted a serious and imminent peril.
As the threat of her fleet had obstructed
Napoleon in 1803, and the Holy Alliance in
1823, so in 1898 it blocked the Kaiser. Late
in that year, when it was all over, the disappointed and baffled Kaiser wrote to a friend
of Joseph Chamberlain, "If I had a larger
fleet I would have taken Uncle Sam by the
scruff of the neck." Have you ever read what
our own fleet was like in those days? Or our
Army? Lucky it was for us that we had to
deal only with Spain. And even the Spanish
fleet would have been a much graver opponent

in Manila Bay, but for Lord Cromer. On its
way from Spain through the Suez Canal a
formidable part of Spain's navy stopped to
coal at Port Said. There is a law about the
coaling of belligerent warships in neutral
ports. Lord Cromer could have construed
that law just as well against us. His construc-
tion brought it about that those Spanish ships
couldn't get to Manila Bay in time to take
part against Admiral Dewey. The Spanish
War revealed that our Navy could hit eight
times out of a hundred, and was in other
respects unprepared and utterly inadequate
to cope with a first-class power. In consequence of this, and the criticisms of our Navy
Department, which Admiral Sims as a young
man had written, Roosevelt took the steps he
did in his first term. Three ticklish times in
that Spanish War England stood our friend
against Germany. When it broke out, German
agents approached Mr. Balfour, proposing
that England join in a European combination
in Spain's favor. Mr. Balfour's refusal is
common knowledge, except to the mono-
maniac with his complex. Next came the action of Lord Cromer, and finally that moment
in Manila Bay when England took her stand
by our side and Germany saw she would have
to fight us both, if she fought at all.

If you saw any German or French papers at the time of our troubles with Spain, you saw undisguised hostility. If you have talked with any American who was in Paris during that April of 1898, your impression will be more vivid still. There was an outburst of European hate for us. Germany, France, and Austria all looked expectantly to England— and England disappointed their expectations. The British press was as much for us as the French and German press were hostile; the London *Spectator* said: "We are not, and we do not pretend to be, an agreeable people, but when there is trouble in the family, we know where our hearts are."

In those same days (somewhere about the third week in April, 1898), at the British Embassy in Washington, occurred a scene of significance and interest, which has probably been told less often than that interview between Mr. Balfour and the Kaiser's emissary in London. The British Ambassador was standing at his window, looking out at the German Embassy, across the street. With him was a member of his diplomatic household. The two watched what was happening. One by one, the representatives of various European nations were entering the door of the German Embassy. "Do you see them?"

said the Ambassador's companion; "they'll all be in there soon. There! That's the last of them." "I didn't notice the French Ambassador." "Yes, he's gone in, too." "I'm surprised at that. I'm sorry for that. I didn't think he would be one of them," said the British Ambassador. "Now, I'll tell you what. They'll all be coming over here in a little while. I want you to wait and be present." Shortly this prediction was verified. Over from the German Embassy came the whole company on a visit to the British Ambassador, that he might add his signature to a document to which they had affixed theirs. He read it quietly. We may easily imagine its purport, since we know of the meditated European coalition against us at the time of our war with Spain. Then the British Ambassador remarked: "I have no orders from my Government to sign any such document as that. And if I did have, I should resign my post rather than sign it." A pause: The company fell silent. "Then what will your Excellency do?" inquired one visitor. "If you will all do me the honor of coming back tomorrow, I shall have another document ready which all of us can sign." That is what happened to the European coalition at this end.

Some few years later, that British Ambassador came to die; and to the British Embassy repaired Theodore Roosevelt. "Would it be possible for us to arrange," he said, "a funeral more honored and marked than the United States has ever accorded to any one not a citizen? I should like it. And," he suddenly added, shaking his fist at the German Embassy over the way, "I'd like to grind all their noses in the dirt."

Confronted with the awkward fact that Britain was almost unanimously with us, from Mr. Balfour down through the British press to the British people, those nations whose ambassadors had paid so unsuccessful a call at the British Embassy had to give it up. Their coalition never came off. Such a thing couldn't come off without England, and England said No.

Next, Lord Cromer, at Port Said, stretched out the arm of international law, and laid it upon the Spanish fleet. Belligerents may legally take coal enough at neutral ports to reach their nearest "home port." That Spanish fleet was on its way from Spain to Manila through the Suez Canal. It could have reached there, had Lord Cromer allowed it coal enough to make the nearest home port *ahead* of it—Manila. But there was a home port *behind* it, still nearer, namely, Barcelona. He let it take coal enough to get back to Barcelona. Thus, England again stepped in.

The third time was in Manila Bay itself, after Dewey's victory, and while he was in occupation of the place. Once more the Kaiser tried it, not discouraged by his failure with Mr. Balfour and the British Government. He desired the Philippines for himself; we had not yet acquired them; we were policing them, superintending the harbor, administering whatever had fallen to us from Spain's defeat. The Kaiser sent, under Admiral Diedrich, a squadron stronger than Dewey's. Dewey indicated where the German was to anchor. "I am here by the order of his Majesty the German Emperor," said Diedrich, and chose his own place to anchor. He made it quite plain in other ways that he was taking no orders from America. Dewey, so report has it, at last told him that "if he wanted a fight he could have it at the drop of the hat." Then it was that the German called on the English Admiral, Chichester, who was likewise on hand, anchored in Manila Bay. "What would you do," inquired Diedrich, "in the event of trouble between Admiral Dewey

and myself?" "That is a secret known only
to Admiral Dewey and me," said the Englishman. Plainer talk could hardly be. Diedrich,
though a German, understood it. He returned
to his flagship. What he saw next morning
was the British cruiser in a new place, inter-
posed between Dewey and himself. Once
more, he understood; and he and his squadron
sailed off; and it was soon after this incident
that the disappointed Kaiser wrote that, if
only his fleet had been larger, he would have
taken us by the scruff of the neck.

Tell these things to the next man you hear
talking about George III or the *Alabama*. You
may meet him in front of a bulletin board,
or in a drawing-room. He is amongst us
everywhere, in the street and in the house.
He may be a paid propagandist or merely a
silly, ignorant puppet. But whatever he is,
he will not find much to say in response, unless it be vain, sterile chatter. True come-
back will fail him as it failed that man by the
bulletin board who asked, "What is England
doing, anyhow?" and his neighbor answered,
"Her fleet's keeping the Kaiser out of your
front yard."

XIV

WHAT did England do in the war, anyhow? Let us have these disregarded facts also. From the shelves of history I have pulled down and displayed the facts which our school textbooks have suppressed; I have told the events wherein England has stood our timely friend throughout a century; events which our implanted prejudice leads us to ignore, or to forget; events which show that any one who says England is our hereditary enemy might just about as well say twice two is five.

What did England do in the war, anyhow?

They go on asking it. The propagandists, the prompted puppets, the paid parrots of the press, go on saying these eight senseless words because they are easy to say, since the man who can answer them is generally not there: to every man who is a responsible master of facts we have—well, how many?—irresponsible shouters in this country. What is your experience? How often is it your luck

—as it was mine in front of the bulletin board
—to see a fraud or a fool promptly and satisfactorily put in his place? Make up your
mind that wherever you hear any person
whatsoever, male or female, clean or unclean,
dressed in jeans, or dressed in silks and laces,
inquire what England "did in the war, anyhow?" such person either shirks knowledge,
or else is a fraud or a fool. Tell them what
the man said in the street about the Kaiser
and our front yard, but don't stop there. Tell
them that in May, 1918, England was sending
men of fifty and boys of eighteen and a half
to the front; that in August, 1918, every third
male available between those years was fighting, that eight and a half million men for
army and navy were raised by the British
Empire, of which Ireland's share was two
and three tenths per cent, Wales' three and
seven tenths, Scotland's eight and three
tenths, and England's more than sixty per
cent; and that this, taken proportionately to
our greater population would have amounted
to about thirteen million Americans. When
the war started, the British Empire main-
tained three soldiers out of every 2600 of
the population; her entire army, regular
establishment, reserve and territorial forces,

amounted to seven hundred thousand men. Our casualties were three hundred and twenty-two thousand, one hundred and eighty-two. The casualties in the British Army were three million, forty-nine thousand, nine hundred and seventy-one—a million more than we sent —and of these six hundred and fifty-eight thousand, seven hundred and four, were *killed*. Of her Navy, thirty-three thousand three hundred and sixty-one were killed, six thousand four hundred and five wounded and missing; of her merchant marine fourteen thousand six hundred and sixty-one were killed; a total of forty-eight thousand killed —or ten per cent of all in active service. Some of those of the merchant marine who escaped drowning through torpedoes and mines went back to sea after being torpedoed five, six, and seven times.

What did England do in the war, anyhow?

Through four frightful years she fought with splendor, she suffered with splendor, she held on with splendor. The first battle of Ypres is but one drop in the sea of her epic courage; yet it would fill full a canto of a poem. So spent was Britain's single line, so worn and thin, that after all the men available were brought, gaps remained. No more ammunition was coming to these men, the last rounds had been served. Wet through, heavy with mud, they were shelled for three days to prevent sleep. Many came at last to sleep standing; and being jogged awake when officers of the line passed down the trenches, would salute and instantly be asleep again. On the fourth day, with the Kaiser come to watch them crumble, three lines of Huns, wave after wave of Germany's picked troops, fell and broke upon this single line of British —and it held. The Kaiser, had he known of the exhausted ammunition and the mounded dead, could have walked unarmed to the Channel. But he never knew.

Surgeons being scantier than men at Ypres, one with a compound fracture of the thigh had himself propped up, and thus all day worked on the wounded at the front. He knew it meant death for him. The day over, he let them carry him to the rear, and there, from blood-poisoning, he died. Thus through four frightful years, the British met their duty and their death.

There is the great story of the little penny steamers of the Thames—a story lost amid the gigantic whole. Who will tell it right?

Who will make this drop of perfect valor shine in prose or verse for future eyes to see? Imagine a Hoboken ferry boat, because her country needed her, starting for San Francisco around Cape Horn, and getting there. Some ten or eleven penny steamers under their own steam started from the Thames down the Channel, across the Bay of Biscay, past Gibraltar, and through the submarined Mediterranean for the River Tigris. Boats of shallow draught were urgently needed on the River Tigris. Four or five reached their destination. Where are the rest?

What did England do in the war, anyhow?

During 1917–1918 Britain's armies held the enemy in three continents and on six fronts, and coöperated with her Allies on two more fronts. Her dead, those six hundred and fifty-eight thousand dead, lay by the Tigris, the Zambesi, the Ægean, and across the world to Flanders' fields. Between March 21st and April 17th, 1918, the Huns in their drive used 127 divisions, and of these 102 were concentrated against the British. That was in Flanders. Britain, at the same time she was fighting in Flanders, had also at various times shared in the fighting in Russia, Kiaochau,

New Guinea, Samoa, Mesopotamia, Palestine, Egypt, the Sudan, Cameroons, Togoland, East Africa, South West Africa, Saloniki, Aden, Persia, and the northwest frontier of India. Britain cleared twelve hundred thousand square miles of the enemy in German colonies. While fighting in Mesopotamia, her soldiers were reconstructing at the same time. They reclaimed and cultivated more than 1100 square miles of land there, which produced in consequence enough food to save two million tons of shipping annually for the Allies. In Palestine and Mesopotamia alone, British troops in 1917 took 23,590 prisoners. In 1918, in Palestine from September 18th to October 7th, they took 79,000 prisoners.

What did England do in the war, anyhow?

With "French's contemptible little army" she saved France at the start—but I'll skip that—except to mention that one division lost 10,000 out of 12,000 men, and 350 out of 400 officers. At Zeebrugge and Ostend—do not forget the *Vindictive*—she dealt with submarines in April and May, 1918—but I'll skip that; I cannot set down all that she did, either at the start, or nearing the finish, or at any particular moment during those four

years and three months that she was helping
to hold Germany off from the throat of the
world; it would make a very thick book. But
I am giving you enough, I think, wherewith
to answer the ignorant, and the frauds, and
the fools. Tell them that from 1916 to 1918
Great Britain increased her tillage area by
four million acres: wheat 39 per cent, barley
11, oats 35, potatoes 50—in spite of the short-
age of labor. She used wounded soldiers, college boys and girls, boy scouts, refugees, and
she produced the biggest grain crop in *fifty
years.* She started fourteen hundred thousand
new war gardens; most of those who worked
them had worked already a long day in a
munition factory. These devoted workers increased the potato crop in 1917 by three million tons—and thus released British provision
ships to carry our soldiers across. In that
Boston speech which one of my correspondents referred to, our Secretary of the Navy
did not mention this. Mention it yourself.
And tell them about the boy scouts and the
women. Fifteen thousand of the boy scouts
joined the colors, and over fifty thousand of
the younger members served in various ways
at home.

Of England's women seven million were en-

gaged in work on munitions and other neces-
saries and apparatus of war. The terrible
test of that first battle of Ypres, to which I
have made brief allusion above, wrought an
industrial revolution in the manufacture of
shells. The energy of production rose at a
rate which may be indicated by two or three
comparisons: In 1917 as many heavy howitzer
shells were turned out in a single day as in
the whole first year of the war, as many
medium shells in five days, and as many field-
gun shells in eight days. Or in other words,
45 times as many field-gun shells, 73 times as
many medium, and 365 times as many heavy
howitzer shells, were turned out in 1917 as in
the first year of the war. These shells were
manufactured in buildings totaling fifteen
miles in length, forty feet in breadth, with
more than ten thousand machine tools driven
by seventeen miles of shafting with an energy
of twenty-five thousand horse-power and a
weekly output of over ten thousand tons'
weight of projectiles—all this largely worked
by the women of England. While the fleet had
increased its personnel from 136,000 to about
400,000, and 2,000,000 men by July, 1915, had
voluntarily enlisted in the army before England gave up her birthright and accepted com-

pulsory service, the women of England left
their ordinary lives to fabricate the neces-
saries of war. They worked at home while
their husbands, brothers, and sons fought and
died on six battle fronts abroad—six hundred
and fifty-eight thousand died, remember; do
you remember the number of Americans
killed in action?—less than thirty-six thousand;—those English women worked on,
seven millions of them at least, on milk carts,
motor-busses, elevators, steam engines, and in
making ammunition. Never before had any
woman worked on more than 150 of the 500
different processes that go to the making of
munitions. They now handled T. N. T., and
fulminate of mercury, more deadly still;
helped build guns, gun carriages, and three-
and-a-half ton army camions; worked over-
head traveling cranes for moving the boilers
of battleships; turned lathes, made every part
of an aeroplane.

And who were these seven million women?
The eldest daughter of a duke and the daughter of a general won distinction in advanced
munition work. The only daughter of an old
Army family broke down after a year's work
in a base hospital in France, was ordered six
months' rest at home, but after two months

entered a munition factory as an ordinary employee and after nine months' work had lost but five minutes working time. The mother of seven enlisted sons went into munitions not to be behind them in serving England, and one of them wrote her she was probably killing more Germans than any of the family. The stewardess of a torpedoed passenger ship was among the few survivors. Reaching land, she got a job at a capstan lathe. Those were the seven million women of England—daughters of dukes, torpedoed stewardesses, and everything between.

Seven hundred thousand of these were engaged on munition work proper. They did from 60 to 70 per cent of all the machine work on shells, fuses, and trench warfare supplies, and 1450 of them were trained mechanics to the Royal Flying Corps. They were employed upon practically every operation in factory, in foundry, in laboratory, and chemical works, of which they were physically capable; in making of gauges, forging billets, making fuses, cartridges, bullets—"look what they can do," said a foreman, "ladies from homes where they sat about and were waited upon." They also made optical glass; drilled and tapped in the shipyards; renewed electric wires and fittings, wound armatures; lacquered guards for lamps and radiator fronts; repaired junction and section boxes, fire control instruments, automatic searchlights. "We can hardly believe our eyes," said another foreman, "when we see the heavy stuff brought to and from the shops in motor lorries driven by girls. Before the war it was all carted by horses and men. The girls do the job all right, though, and the only thing they ever complain about is that their toes get cold." They worked without hesitation from twelve to fourteen hours a day, or a night, for seven days a week, and with the voluntary sacrifice of public holidays.

That is not all, or nearly all, that the women of England did—I skip their welfare work, recreation work, nursing—but it is enough wherewith to answer the ignorant, or the fraud, or the fool.

What did England do in the war, anyhow?

On August 8, 1914, Lord Kitchener asked for 100,000 volunteers. He had them within fourteen days. In the first week of September 175,000 men enrolled, 30,000 in a single day. Eleven months later, two million had enlisted. Ten months later, five million and forty-one thousand had voluntarily enrolled in the Army and Navy.

In 1914 Britain had in her Royal Naval Air Service 64 aeroplanes and 800 airmen. In 1917 she had many thousand aeroplanes and 42,000 airmen. In her Royal Flying Corps she had in 1914, 66 planes and 100 men; in 1917, several thousand planes and men by tens of thousands. In the first nine months of 1917 British airmen brought down 876 enemy machines and drove down 759 out of control. From July, 1917, to June, 1918, 4102 enemy machines were destroyed or brought down with a loss of 1213 machines.

Besides financing her own war costs she had by October, 1917, loaned eight hundred million dollars to the Dominions and five billion five hundred million to the Allies. She raised five billion in thirty days. In the first eight months of 1918 she contributed to the various forms of war loan at the average rate of one hundred and twenty-four million, eight hundred thousand a week.

Is that enough? Enough to show what England did in the war? No, it is not enough for such people as continue to ask what she did. Nothing would suffice these persons. During the earlier stages of the war it was possible

that the question could be asked honestly—
though never intelligently—because the facts
and figures were not at that time always
accessible. They were still piling up, they
were scattered about, mention of them was
incidental and fugitive, they could be missed
by anybody who was not diligently alert to
find them. To-day it is quite otherwise. The
facts and figures have been compiled, arranged, published in accessible and convenient form; therefore to-day, the man or
woman who persists in asking what England
did in the war is not honest but dishonest or
mentally spotted, and does not want to be
answered. They don't want to know. The
question is merely a camouflage of their spite,
and were every item given of the gigantic and
magnificent contribution that England made
to the defeat of the Kaiser and all his works,
it would not stop their evil mouths. Not for
them am I here setting forth a part of what
England did; it is for the convenience of the
honest American, who does want to know,
that my collection of facts is made from the
various sources which he may not have the
time or the means to look up for himself. For
his benefit I add some particulars concerning
the British Navy which kept the Kaiser out
of our front yard.

Admiral Mahan said in his book—and he was an American of whose knowledge and wisdom Congress seems to have known nothing and cared less—''Why do English innate political conceptions of popular representative government, of the balance of law and liberty, prevail in North America from the Arctic Circle to the Gulf of Mexico, from the Atlantic to the Pacific? Because the command of the sea at the decisive era belonged to Great Britain.'' We have seen that the decisive era was when Napoleon's mouth watered for Louisiana, and when England took her stand behind the Monroe Doctrine.

Admiral Sims said in the second installment of his narrative *The Victory at Sea,* published in *The World's Work* for October, 1919, at page 619: ''. . . Let us suppose for a moment that an earthquake, or some other great natural disturbance, had engulfed the British fleet at Scapa Flow. The world would then have been at Germany's mercy and all the destroyers the Allies could have put upon the sea would have availed them nothing, for the German battleships and battle cruisers could have sunk them or driven them into their ports. Then Allied commerce would have been the prey, not only of the submarines, which could have operated with the utmost freedom, but of the German surface craft as well. In a few weeks the British food supplies would have been exhausted. There would have been an early end to the soldiers and munitions which Britain was constantly sending to France. The United States could have sent no forces to the Western front, and the result would have been the surrender which the Allies themselves, in the spring of 1917, regarded as a not remote possibility. America would then have been compelled to face the German power alone, and to face it long before we had had an opportunity to assemble our resources and equip our armies. The world was preserved from all these calamities because the destroyer and the convoy solved the problem of the submarines, and because back of these agencies of victory lay Admiral Beatty's squadrons, holding at arm's length the German surface ships while these comparatively fragile craft were saving the liberties of the world.''

Yes. The High Seas Fleet of Germany, costing her one billion five hundred million dollars, was bottled up. Five million five hundred thousand tons of German shipping and one million tons of Austrian shipping were driven off the seas or captured; oversea trade and oversea colonies were cut off. Two million oversea Huns of fighting age were hindered from joining the enemy. Ocean commerce and communication were stopped for the Huns and secured to the Allies. In 1916, 2100 mines were swept up and 89 mine sweepers lost. These mine sweepers and patrol boats numbered 12 in 1914, and 3300 by 1918. To patrol the seas British ships had to steam eight million miles in a single month. During the four years of the war they transported oversea more than thirteen million men (losing but 2700 through enemy action) as well as transporting two million horses and mules, five hundred thousand vehicles, twenty-five million tons of explosives, fifty-one million tons of oil and fuel, one hundred and thirty million tons of food and other materials for the use of the Allies. In one month three hundred and fifty-five thousand men were carried from England to France.

It was after Mr. Daniels, Secretary of the Navy, in his speech in Boston to which allusion has been made, had given our navy all and the British navy none of the credit of conveying our soldiers overseas, that Admiral Sims repaired the singular oblivion of the Secretary. We Americans should know the truth, he said. We had not been too accurately informed. We did not seem to have been told by anybody, for instance, that of the five thousand anti-submarine craft operating day and night in the infested waters, we had 160, or 3 per cent; that of the million and a half troops which had gone over from here in a few months, Great Britain brought over two thirds and escorted half.

"I would like American papers to pay particular attention to the fact that there are about 5000 anti-submarine craft in the ocean to-day, cutting out mines, escorting troop ships, and making it possible for us to go ahead and win this war. They can do this because the British Grand Fleet is so powerful that the German High Seas Fleet has to stay at home. The British Grand Fleet is the foundation stone of the cause of the whole of the Allies."

Thus Admiral Sims.

That is part of what England did in the war.

NOTE.—The author expresses thanks and acknowledgment to *Pearson's Magazine* for permission to use the passages quoted from the articles by Admiral Sims.

RUDE BRITANNIA, CRUDE COLUMBIA

IT may have been ten years ago, it may have been fifteen—and just how long it was before the war makes no matter—that I received an invitation to join a society for the promotion of more friendly relations between the United States and England.

"No, indeed," I said to myself.

Even as I read the note, hostility rose in me. Refusal sprang to my lips before my reason had acted at all. I remembered George III. I remembered the Civil War. The ancient grudge, the anti-English complex, had been instantly set fermenting in me. Nothing could better disclose its lurking persistence than my virtually automatic exclamation, "No, indeed!" I knew something about England's friendly acts, about Venezuela, and Manila Bay, and Edmund Burke, and John Bright, and the Queen, and the Lancashire cotton spinners. And more than this historic knowledge, I knew living English people, men and women, among whom I counted dear and even beloved friends. I knew also, just as well as Admiral Mahan knew, and other Americans by the hundreds of thousands have known and know at this moment, that all the best we have and are—law, ethics, love of liberty—all of it came from England, grew in England first, ripened from the seed of which we are merely one great harvest, planted here by England. And yet I instantly exclaimed, "No, indeed!"

Well, having been inflicted with the anti-English complex myself, I understand it all the better in others, and am begging them to counteract it as I have done. You will recollect that I said at the outset of these observations that, as I saw it, our prejudice was founded upon three causes fairly separate, although they often melted together. With two of these causes I have now dealt—the school histories, and certain acts and policies of England's throughout our relations with her. The third cause, I said, was certain traits of the English and ourselves which have produced personal friction. An American does or says something which angers an Englishman, who thereupon goes about thinking and saying, "Those insufferable Yankees!" An Englishman does or says something which angers an American, who thereupon goes about thinking and saying, "To Hell with England!" Each makes the well-nigh universal—but none the less perfectly ridiculous —blunder of damning a whole people because one of them has rubbed him the wrong way. Nothing could show up more forcibly and vividly this human weakness for generalizing from insufficient data, than the incident in London streets which I promised to tell you in full when we should reach the time for it. The time is now.

In a hospital at no great distance from San Francisco, a wounded American soldier said to one who sat beside him, that never would he go to Europe to fight anybody again—except the English. Them he would like to fight; and to the astonished visitor he told his reason. He, it appeared, was one of our Americans who marched through London streets on that day when the eyes of London looked for the first time upon the Yankees at last arrived to bear a hand to England and her Allies. From the mob came a certain taunt:

"You silly ass."

It was, as you will observe, an unflattering interpretation of our national initials, U. S. A. Of course it was enough to make a proper American doughboy entirely "hot under the collar." To this reading of our national initials our national readiness retorted in kind at an early date: A. E. F. meant After England Failed. But why, months and months afterwards, when everything was over, did that foolish doughboy in the hospital hug this lone thing to his memory? It was the act of an unthinking few. Didn't he notice what the rest of London was doing that day? Didn't he remember that she flew the Union Jack and the Stars and Stripes together from every symbolic pinnacle of creed and government that rose above her continent of streets and dwellings to the sky? Couldn't he feel that England, his old enemy and old mother, bowed and stricken and struggling, was opening her arms to him wide? She's a person who hides her tears even from herself; but it seems to me that, with a drop of imagination and half a drop of thought, he might have discovered a year and a half after a few street roughs had insulted him, that they were not all England. With two drops of thought it might even have ultimately struck him that here we came, late, very late, indeed, only just in time, from a country untouched, unafflicted, unbombed, safe, because of England's ships, to tired, broken, bleeding England; and that the sight of us, so jaunty, so fresh, so innocent of suffering and bereavement should have been for a thoughtless moment galling to unthinking brains?

I am perfectly sure that if such considerations as these were laid before any American soldier who still smarted under that taunt in London streets, his good American sense, which is our best possession, would grasp and accept the thing in its true proportions. He wouldn't want to blot an Empire out because a handful of muckers called him names. Of this I am perfectly sure, because in Paris streets it was my happy lot four months after the Armistice to talk with many American soldiers, among whom some felt sore about the French. Not one of these but saw with his good American sense, directly I pointed certain facts out to him, that his hostile generalization had been unjust. But, to quote the oft-quoted Mr. Kipling, that is another story.

An American regiment just arrived in France was encamped for purposes of training and experience next a British regiment come back from the front to rest. The streets of the two camps were adjacent, and the Tommies walked out to watch the Yankees pegging down their tents.

"Aw," they said, "wot a shyme you've brought nobody along to tuck you in."

They made other similar remarks; commented unfavorably upon the alignment; "You were a bit late in coming," they said. Of course our boys had answers, and to these the Tommies had further answers, and this encounter of wits very naturally led to a result which could not possibly have been happier. I don't know what the Tommies expected the Yankees to do. I suppose they were as ignorant of our nature as we of theirs, and that they entertained preconceived notions. They suddenly found that we were, once again to quote Mr. Kipling, "bachelors in barricks most remarkable like" themselves. An American first sergeant hit a British first sergeant. Instantly a thousand men were milling. For thirty minutes they kept at it. Warriors reeled together and fell and rose and got it in the neck and the jaw and the eye and the nose—and all the while the British and American officers, splendidly discreet, saw none of it. British soldiers were carried back to their streets, still fighting, bunged Yankees staggered everywhere—but not an officer saw any of it. Black eyes the next day, and other tokens, very plainly showed who had been at this party. Thereafter a much better feeling prevailed between Tommies and Yanks.

A more peaceful contact produced excellent consequences at an encampment of Americans in England. The Americans had brought over an idea, apparently, that the English were "easy." They tried it on in sundry ways, but ended by the discovery that, while engaged upon this enterprise, they had been in sundry ways quite completely "done" themselves. This gave them a respect for their English cousins which they had never felt before.

Here is another tale, similar in moral. This occurred at Brest, in France. In the Y hut sat an English lady, one of the hostesses. To her came a young American marine with whom she already had some acquaintance. This led him to ask for her advice. He said to her that as his permission was of only seventy-two hours, he wanted to be as economical of his time as he could and see everything best worth while for him to see during his leave. Would she, therefore, tell him what things in Paris were the most interesting and in what order he had best take them? She replied with another suggestion; why not, she said, ask permission for England? This would give him two weeks instead of seventy-two hours. At this he burst out violently that he would not set foot in England; that he never wanted to have anything to do with England or with the English: "Why, I am a marine!" he exclaimed, "and we marines would sooner knock down any English sailor than speak to him."

The English lady, naturally, did not then tell him her nationality. She now realized that he had supposed her to be American, because she had frequently been in America and had talked to him as no stranger to the country could. She, of course, did not urge his going to England; she advised him what to see in France. He took his leave of seventy-two hours and when he returned was very grateful for the advice she had given him. She saw him often after this, and he grew to rely very much upon her friendly counsel. Finally, when the time came for her to go away from Brest, she told him that she was English. And then she said something like this to him:

"Now, you told me you had never been in England and had never known an English person in your life, and yet you had all these ideas against us because somebody had taught you wrong. It is not all your fault. You are only nineteen years old and you cannot read about us, because you have no chance; but at least you do know one English person now, and that English person begs you, when you do have a chance to read and inform yourself of the truth, to find out what England really has been, and what she has really done in this war.''

The end of the story is that the boy, who had become devoted to her, did as she suggested. To-day she receives letters from him which show that nothing is left of his anti-English complex. It is another instance of how clearly our native American mind, if only the facts are given it, thinks, judges, and concludes.

It is for those of my countrymen who will never have this chance, never meet some one who can guide them to the facts, that I tell these things. Let them ''cut out the dope.'' At this very moment that I write—November 24, 1919—the dope is being fed freely to all who are ready, whether through ignorance or through interested motives, to swallow it. The ancient grudge is being played up strong over the whole country in the interest of Irish independence.

Ian Hay in his two books so timely and so excellent, *Getting Together* and *The Oppressed English,* could not be as unreserved, naturally, as I can be about those traits in my own countrymen which have, in the past at any rate, retarded English cordiality towards Americans. Of these I shall speak as plainly as I know how. But also, being an American and therefore by birth more indiscreet than Ian Hay, I shall speak as plainly as I know how of those traits in the English which have helped to keep warm our ancient grudge. Thus I may render both countries forever uninhabitable to me, but shall at least take with me into exile a character for strict, if disastrous, impartiality.

I begin with an American who was traveling in an English train. It stopped somewhere, and out of the window he saw some buildings which interested him.

"Can you tell me what those are?" he asked an Englishman, a stranger, who sat in the other corner of the compartment.

"Better ask the guard," said the Englishman.

Since that brief dialogue, this American does not think well of the English.

Now, two interpretations of the English-

man's answer are possible. One is, that he
didn't himself know, and said so in his English way. English talk is often very short,
much shorter than ours. That is because they
all understand each other, are much closer
knit than we are. Behind them are generations of "doing it" in the same established
way, a way that their long experience of life
has hammered out for their own convenience,
and which they like. We're not nearly so
closely knit together here, save in certain
spots, especially the old spots. In Boston they
understand each other with very few words
said. So they do in Charleston. But these
spots of condensed and hoarded understanding lie far apart, are never confluent, and also
differ in their details; while the whole of England is confluent, and the details have been
slowly worked out through centuries of getting on together, and are accepted and observed exactly like the rules of a game.

In America, if the American didn't know,
he would have answered, "I don't know. I
think you'll have to ask the conductor," or at
any rate, his reply would have been longer
than the Englishman's. But I am not going
to accept the idea that the Englishman didn't
know and said so in his brief usual way. It's

equally possible that he did know. Then, you naturally ask, why in the name of common civility did he give such an answer to the American?

I believe that I can tell you. He didn't know that my friend was an American, he thought he was an Englishman who had broken the rules of the game. We do have some rules here in America, only we have not nearly so many, they're much more stretchable, and it's not all of us who have learned them. But nevertheless a good many have.

Suppose you were traveling in a train here, and the man next you, whose face you had never seen before, and with whom you had not yet exchanged a syllable, said: "What's your pet name for your wife?"

Wouldn't your immediate inclination be to say, "What damned business is that of yours?" or words to that general effect?

But again, you most naturally object, there was nothing personal in my friend's question about the buildings. No; but that is not it. At the bottom, both questions are an invasion of the same deep-seated thing—*the right to privacy*. In America, what with the newspaper reporters and this and that and the other, the territory of a man's privacy has been lessened and lessened until very little of it remains; but most of us still do draw the line somewhere; we may not all draw it at the same place, but we do draw a line. The difference, then, between ourselves and the English in this respect is simply, that with them the territory of a man's privacy covers more ground, and different ground as well. An Englishman doesn't expect strangers to ask him questions of a guidebook sort. For all such questions his English system provides perfectly definite persons to answer. If you want to know where the ticket office is, or where to take your baggage, or what time the train goes, or what platform it starts from, or what towns it stops at, and what churches or other buildings of interest are to be seen in those towns, there are porters and guards and Bradshaws and guidebooks to tell you, and it's they whom you are expected to consult, not any fellow-traveler who happens to be at hand. If you ask him, you break the rules. Had my friend said: "I am an American. Would you mind telling me what those buildings are?" all would have gone well. The Englishman would have recognized (not fifty years ago, but certainly to-day) that it wasn't a question of rules between them, and would have at once explained—either that he didn't know, or that the buildings were such and such.

Do not, I beg, suppose for a moment that I am holding up the English way as better than our own—or worse. I am not making comparisons; I am trying to show differences. Very likely there are many points wherein we think the English might do well to borrow from us; and it is quite as likely that the English think we might here and there take a leaf from their book to our advantage. But I am not theorizing, I am not seeking to show that we manage life better or that they manage life better; the only moral that I seek to draw from these anecdotes is, that we should each understand and hence make allowance for the other fellow's way. You will admit, I am sure, be you American or English, that everybody has a right to his own way? The proverb "When in Rome you must do as Rome does" covers it, and would save trouble if we always obeyed it. The people who forget it most are they that go to Rome for the first time; and I shall give you both English and American examples of this presently. It is good to ascertain before you go to Rome, if you can, what Rome does do.

Have you never been mistaken for a waiter, or something of that sort? Perhaps you will have heard the anecdote about one of our ambassadors to England. All ambassadors, save ours, wear on formal occasions a distinguishing uniform, just as our army and navy officers do; it is convenient, practical, and saves trouble. But we have declared it menial, or despotic, or un-American, or something equally silly, and hence our ambassadors must wear evening dress resembling closely the attire of those who are handing the supper or answering the door-bell. An Englishman saw Mr. Choate at some diplomatic function, standing about in this evening costume, and said:

"Call me a cab."

"You are a cab," said Mr. Choate, obediently.

Thus did he make known to the Englishman that he was not a waiter. Similarly in crowded hotel dining-rooms or crowded railroad stations have agitated ladies clutched my arm and said:

"I want a table for three," or "When does the train go to Poughkeepsie?"

Just as we in America have regular people to attend to these things, so do they in England; and as the English respect each other's right to privacy very much more than we do, they resent invasions of it very much more than we do. But, let me say again, they are likely to mind it only in somebody they think knows the rules. With those who don't know them it is different. I say this with all the more certainty because of a fairly recent afternoon spent in an English garden with English friends. The question of pronunciation came up. Now you will readily see that with them and their compactness, their great public schools, their two great Universities, and their great London, the one eternal focus of them all, both the chance of diversity in social customs and the tolerance of it must be far less than in our huge unfocused country. With us, Boston, New York, Philadelphia, Chicago, San Francisco, is each a centre. Here you can pronounce the word calm, for example, in one way or another, and it merely indicates where you come from. Departure in England from certain established pronunciations has another effect.

"Of course," said one of my friends, "one knows where to place anybody who says 'girl'" (pronouncing it as it is spelled).

"That's frightful," said I, "because I say 'girl'."

"Oh, but you are an American. It doesn't apply."

But had I been English, it would have been something like coming to dinner without your collar.

That is why I think that, had my friend in the train begun his question about the buildings by saying that he was an American, the answer would have been different. Not all the English yet, but many more than there were fifty or even twenty years ago, have ceased to apply their rules to us.

About 1874 a friend of mine from New York was taken to a London club. Into the room where he was came the Prince of Wales, who took out a cigar, felt for and found no matches, looked about, and there was a silence. My friend thereupon produced matches, struck one, and offered it to the Prince, who bowed, thanked him, lighted his cigar, and presently went away.

Then an Englishman observed to my friend: "It's not the thing for a commoner to offer a light to the Prince."

"I'm not a commoner, I'm an American," said my friend with perfect good nature.

Whatever their rule may be to-day about the Prince and matches, as to us they have come to accept my friend's pertinent distinction: they don't expect us to keep or even to know their own set of rules.

Indeed, they surpass us in this, they make more allowances for us than we for them. They don't criticize Americans for not being English. Americans still constantly do criticize the English for not being Americans. Now, the measure in which you *don't* allow for the customs of another country is the measure of your own provincialism. I have heard some of our own soldiers express dislike of the English because of their coldness. The English are not cold; they are silent upon certain matters. But it is all there. Do you remember that sailor at Zeebrugge carrying the unconscious body of a comrade to safety, not sure yet if he were alive or dead, and stroking that comrade's head as he went, saying over and over, "Did you think I would leave yer?" We are more demonstrative, we spell things out which it is the way of the English to leave between the lines. But it is all there! Behind that unconciliating wall of shyness and reserve, beats and hides the warm, loyal British heart, the most constant heart in the world.

"It isn't done."

That phrase applies to many things in England besides offering a light to the Prince, or asking a fellow traveler what those buildings are; and I think that the Englishman's notion of his right to privacy lies at the bottom of quite a number of these things. You may lay some of them to snobbishness, to caste, to shyness, they may have various secondary origins; but I prefer to cover them all with the broader term, the right to privacy, because it seems philosophically to account for them and explain them.

In May, 1915, an Oxford professor was in New York. A few years before this I had read a book of his which had delighted me. I met him at lunch, I had not known him before. Even as we shook hands, I blurted out to him my admiration for his book.

"Oh."

That was the whole of his reply. It made me laugh at myself, for I should have known better. I had often been in England and could have told anybody that you mustn't too abruptly or obviously refer to what the other fellow does, still less to what you do yourself. "It isn't done." It's a sort of indecent exposure. It's one of the invasions of the right to privacy.

In America, not everywhere but in many

places, a man upon entering a club and seeing
a friend across the room, will not hesitate to
call out to him, "Hullo, Jack!" or "Hullo,
George!" or whatever. In England "it isn't
done." The greeting would be conveyed by
a short nod or a glance. To call out a man's
name across a room full of people, some of
whom may be total strangers, invades his
privacy and theirs. Have you noticed how,
in our Pullman parlor cars, a party sitting
together, generally young women, will shriek
their conversation in a voice that bores like a
gimlet through the whole place? That is an
invasion of privacy. In England "it isn't
done." We shouldn't stand it in a theatre,
but in parlor cars we do stand it. It is a good
instance to show that the Englishman's right
to privacy is larger than ours, and thus that
his liberty is larger than ours.

Before leaving this point, which to my
thinking is the cause of many frictions and
misunderstandings between ourselves and the
English, I mustn't omit to give instances of
divergence, where an Englishman will speak
of matters upon which we are silent, and is
silent upon subjects of which we will speak.

You may present a letter of introduction to
an Englishman, and he wishes to be civil, to

help you to have a good time. It is quite possible he may say something like this:

"I think you had better know my sister Sophy. You mayn't like her. But her dinners are rather amusing. Of course the food's ghastly because she's the stingiest woman in London."

On the other hand, many Americans (though less willing than the French) are willing to discuss creed, immortality, faith. There is nothing from which the Englishman more peremptorily recoils, although he hates well nigh as deeply all abstract discussion, or to be clever, or to have you be clever. An American friend of mine had grown tired of an Englishman who had been finding fault with one American thing after another. So he suddenly said:

"Will you tell me why you English when you enter your pews on Sunday always immediately smell your hats?"

The Englishman stiffened. "I refuse to discuss religious subjects with you," he said.

To be ponderous over this anecdote grieves me—but you may not know that orthodox Englishmen usually don't *kneel*, as we do, after reaching their pews; they *stand* for a moment, covering their faces with their well-brushed hats: with each nation the observance is the same, it is in the manner of the observing that we differ.

Much is said about our "common language," and its being a reason for our understanding each other. Yes; but it is also almost as much a cause for our misunderstanding each other. It is both a help and a trap. If we Americans spoke something so wholly different from English as French is, comparisons couldn't be made; and somebody has remarked that comparisons are odious.

"Why do you call your luggage baggage?" says the Englishman—or used to say.

"Why do you call your baggage luggage?" says the American—or used to say.

"Why don't you say treacle?" inquires the Englishman.

"Because we call it molasses," answers the American.

"How absurd to speak of a car when you mean a carriage!" exclaims the Englishman.

"We don't mean a carriage, we mean a car," retorts the American.

You, my reader, may have heard (or perhaps even held) foolish conversations like that; and you will readily perceive that if we didn't say "car" when we spoke of the vehicle you get into when you board a train, but called it a *voiture,* or something else quite "foreign," the Englishman would not feel that we had taken a sort of liberty with his mother-tongue. A deep point lies here: for most English the world is divided into three peoples, English, foreigners and Americans; and for most of us likewise it is divided into Americans, foreigners, and English. Now a "foreigner" can call molasses whatever he pleases; we do not feel that he has taken any liberty with our mother-tongue; his tongue has a different mother; he can't help that; he's not to be criticized for that. But we and the English speak a tongue *that has the same mother.* This identity in pedigree has led and still leads to countless family discords. I've not a doubt that divergences in vocabulary and in accent were the fount and origin of some swollen noses, some battered eyes, when our Yankees mixed with the Tommies. Each would be certain to think that the other couldn't "talk straight"—and each would be certain to say so. I shall not here spin out a list of different names for the same things now current in English and American usage: molasses and treacle will suffice for an example; you will be able easily to think of others, and there are many such that occur in everyday speech. Almost more tricky are those words which both peoples use alike, but with different meanings. I shall spin no list of these either; one example there is which I cannot name, of two words constantly used in both countries, each word quite proper in one country, while in the other it is more than improper. Thirty years ago I explained this one evening to a young Englishman who was here for a while. Two or three days later, he thanked me fervently for the warning: it had saved him, during a game of tennis, from a frightful shock, when his partner, a charming girl, meaning to tell him to cheer up, had used the word that is so harmless with us and in England so far beyond the pale of polite society.

Quite as much as words, accent also leads to dissension. I have heard many an American speak of the English accent as "affected"; and our accent displeases the English. Now what Englishman, or what American, ever criticizes a Frenchman for not pronouncing our language as we do? His tongue has a different mother!

I know not how in the course of the years all these divergences should have come about, and none of us need care. There they are.

As a matter of fact, both England and America are mottled with varying accents literate and illiterate; equally true it is that each nation has its notion of the other's way of speaking —we're known by our shrill nasal twang, they by their broad vowels and hesitation; and quite as true is it that not all Americans and not all English do in their enunciation conform to these types.

One May afternoon in 1919 I stopped at Salisbury to see that beautiful cathedral and its serene and gracious close. "Star-scattered on the grass," and beneath the noble trees, lay New Zealand soldiers, solitary or in little groups, gazing, drowsing, talking at ease. Later, at the inn I was shown to a small table, where sat already a young Englishman in evening dress, at his dinner. As I sat down opposite him, I bowed, and he returned it. Presently we were talking. When I said that I was stopping expressly to see the cathedral, and how like a trance it was to find a scene so utterly English full of New Zealanders lying all about, he looked puzzled. It was at this, or immediately after this, that I explained to him my nationality.

"I shouldn't have known it," he remarked, after an instant's pause.

I pressed him for his reason, which he

gave; somewhat reluctantly, I think, but with excellent good-will. Of course it was the same old mother-tongue!

"You mean," I said, "that I haven't happened to say 'I guess,' and that I don't, perhaps, talk through my nose? But we don't all do that. We do all sorts of things."

He stuck to it. "You talk like us."

"Well, I'm sure I don't mean to talk like anybody!" I sighed.

This diverted him, and brought us closer.

"And see here," I continued, "I knew you were English, although you've not dropped a single h."

"Oh, but," he said, "dropping h's—that's —that's not—"

"I know it isn't," I said. "Neither is talking through your nose. And we don't all say 'Amurrican.' "

But he stuck to it. "All the same there *is* an American voice. The train yesterday was full of it. Officers. Unmistakable." And he shook his head.

After this we got on better than ever; and as he went his way, he gave me some advice about the hotel. I should do well to avoid the reading-room. The hotel went in rather too much for being old-fashioned. Ran it into the ground. Tiresome. Good-night.

Presently I shall disclose more plainly to you the moral of my Salisbury anecdote.

Is it their discretion, do you think, that closes the lips of the French when they visit our shores? Not from the French do you hear prompt aspersions as to our differences from them. They observe that proverb about being in Rome: they may not be able to do as Rome does, but they do not inquire why Rome isn't like Paris. If you ask them how they like our hotels or our trains, they may possibly reply that they prefer their own, but they will hardly volunteer this opinion. But the American in England and the Englishman in America go about volunteering opinions. Are the French more discreet? I believe that they are; but I wonder if there is not also something else at the bottom of it. You and I will say things about our cousins to our aunt. Our aunt would not allow outsiders to say those things. Is it this, the-members-of-the-family principle, which makes us less discreet than the French? Is it this, too, which leads us by a seeming paradox to resent criticism *more* when it comes from England? I know not how it may be with you; but with me, when I pick up the paper and read that the Germans are calling us pig-dogs again, I am merely amused. When I read French or Italian abuse of us, I am sorry, to be sure; but when some English paper jumps on us, I hate it, even when I know that what it says isn't true. So here, if I am right in my members-of-the-family hypothesis, you have the English and ourselves feeling free to be disagreeable to each other because we are relations, and yet feeling especially resentful because it's a relation who is being disagreeable. I merely put the point to you, I lay no dogma down concerning members of the family; but I am perfectly sure that discretion is a quality more common to the French than to ourselves or our relations: I mean something a little more than discretion, I mean *esprit de conduite,* for which it is hard to find a translation.

Upon my first two points, the right to privacy and the mother-tongue, I have lingered long, feeling these to be not only of prime importance and wide application, but also to be quite beyond my power to make lucid in short compass. I trust that they have been made lucid. I must now get on to further anecdotes, illustrating other and less subtle causes of misunderstanding; and I feel somewhat like the author of Don Juan when he exclaims that he almost wishes he had ne'er begun that very remarkable poem. I renounce all pretense to the French virtue of discretion.

Evening dress has been the source of many irritations. Englishmen did not appear to think that they need wear it at American dinner parties. There was a good deal of this at one time. During that period an Englishman, who had brought letters to a gentleman in Boston and in consequence had been asked to dinner, entered the house of his host in a tweed suit. His host, in evening dress of course, met him in the hall.

"Oh, I see," said the Bostonian, "that you haven't your dress suit with you. The man will take you upstairs and one of mine will fit you well enough. We'll wait."

In England, a cricketer from Philadelphia, after the match at Lord's had been invited to dine at a great house with the rest of his eleven. They were to go there on a coach. The American discovered after arrival that he alone of the eleven had not brought a dress suit with him. He asked his host what he was to do.

"I advise you to go home," said the host.

The moral here is not that all hosts in England would have treated a guest so, or that all American hosts would have met the situa-

tion so well as that Boston gentleman: but too
many English used to be socially brutal—
quite as much so to each other as to us, or any
one. One should bear that in mind. I know
of nothing more English in its way than what
Eton answered to Beaumont (I think) when
Beaumont sent a challenge to play cricket:

"Harrow we know, and Rugby we have
heard of. But who are you?"

That sort of thing belongs rather to the
Palmerston days than to these; belongs to
days that were nearer in spirit to the Waterloo of 1815, which a haughty England won,
than to the Waterloo of 1914–1918, which a
humbler England so nearly lost.

Turn we next the other way for a look
at ourselves. An American lady who had
brought a letter of introduction to an Englishman in London was in consequence asked
to lunch. He naturally and hospitably gathered to meet her various distinguished guests.
Afterwards she wrote him that she wished
him to invite her to lunch again, as she had
matters of importance to tell him. Why, then,
didn't she ask him to lunch with her? Can you
see? I think I do.

An American lady was at a house party in
Scotland at which she met a gentleman of old

and famous Scotch blood. He was wearing the kilt of his clan. While she talked with him she stared, and finally burst out laughing. "I declare," she said, "that's positively the most ridiculous thing I ever saw a man dressed in."

At the Savoy hotel in August, 1914, when England declared war upon Germany, many American women made scenes of confusion and vociferation. About England and the blast of Fate which had struck her they had nothing to say, but crowded and wailed of their own discomforts, meals, rooms, every paltry personal inconvenience to which they were subjected, or feared that they were going to be subjected. Under the unprecedented stress this was, perhaps, not unnatural; but it would have seemed less displeasing had they also occasionally showed concern for England's plight and peril.

An American, this time a man (our crudities are not limited to the sex) stood up in a theatre, disputing the sixpence which you always have to pay for your program in the London theatres. He disputed so long that many people had to stand waiting to be shown their seats.

During deals at a game of bridge on a

Cunard steamer, the talk had turned upon a certain historic house in an English county. The talk was friendly, everything had been friendly each day.

"Well," said a very rich American to his English partner in the game, "those big estates will all be ours pretty soon. We're going to buy them up and turn your island into our summer resort." No doubt this millionaire intended to be playfully humorous.

At a table where several British and one American—an officer—sat during another ocean voyage between Liverpool and Halifax in June, 1919, the officer expressed satisfaction to be getting home again. He had gone over, he said, to "clean up the mess the British had made."

To a company of Americans who had never heard it before, was told the well-known exploit of an American girl in Europe. In an ancient church she was shown the tomb of a soldier who had been killed in battle three centuries ago. In his honor and memory, because he lost his life bravely in a great cause, his family had kept a little glimmering lamp alight ever since. It hung there, beside the tomb.

"And that's never gone out in all this time?" asked the American girl.

"Never," she was told.

"Well, it's out now, anyway," and she blew it out.

All the Americans who heard this were shocked—all but one, who said:

"Well, I think she was right."

There you are! There you have us at our very worst! And with this plump specimen of the American in Europe at his very worst, I turn back to the English: only, pray do not fail to give those other Americans who were shocked by the outrage of the lamp their due. How wide of the mark would you be if you judged us all by the one who approved of that horrible vandal girl's act! It cannot be too often repeated that we must never condemn a whole people for what some of the people do.

In the two-and-a-half anecdotes which follow, you must watch out for something which lies beneath their very obvious surface.

An American sat at lunch with a great English lady in her country-house. Although she had seen him but once before, she began a conversation like this:

Did the American know the van Squibbers?

He did not.

Well, the van Squibbers, his hostess explained, were Americans who lived in London

and went everywhere. One certainly did see
them everywhere. They were almost too extraordinary.

Now the American knew quite all about
these van Squibbers. He knew also that in
New York, and Boston, and Philadelphia,
and in many other places where existed
a society with still some ragged remnants
of decency and decorum left, one would
not meet this highly star-spangled family
"everywhere."

The hostess kept it up. Did the American
know the Butteredbuns? No? Well, one met
the Butteredbuns everywhere too. They were
rather more extraordinary than the van
Squibbers. And then there were the Cake-
walks, and the Smith-Trapezes. Mrs. Smith-
Trapeze wasn't as extraordinary as her
daughter—the one that put the live frog in
Lord Meldon's soup—and of course neither
of them were "talked about" in the same way
that the eldest Cakewalk girl was talked
about. Everybody went to them, of course,
because one really never knew what one might
miss if one didn't go.

At length the American said:

"You must correct me if I am wrong in an
impression I have received. Vulgar Ameri-

cans seem to me to get on very well in London."

The hostess paused for a moment, and then she said:

"That is perfectly true."

This acknowledgment was complete, and perfectly friendly, and after that all went better than it had gone before.

The half anecdote is a part of this one, and happened a few weeks later at table—dinner this time.

Sitting next to the same American was an English lady whose conversation led him to repeat to her what he had said to his hostess at lunch: "Vulgar Americans seem to get on very well in London society."

"They do," said the lady, "and I will tell you why. We English—I mean that set of English—are blasé. We see each other too much, we are all alike in our ways, and we are awfully tired of it. Therefore it refreshes us and amuses us to see something new and different."

"Then," said the American, "you accept these hideous people's invitations, and go to their houses, and eat their food, and drink their champagne, and it's just like going to see the monkeys at the Zoo?"

"It is," returned the lady.

"But," the American asked, "isn't that awfully low down of you?" (He smiled as he said it.)

Immediately the English lady assented; and grew more cordial. When next day the party came to break up, she contrived in the manner of her farewell to make the American understand that because of their conversation she bore him not ill will but good will.

Once more, the scene of my anecdote is at table, a long table in a club, where men came to lunch. All were Englishmen, except a single stranger. He was an American, who through the kindness of one beloved member of that club, no longer living now, had received a card to the club. The American, upon sitting down alone in this company, felt what I suppose that many of us feel in like circumstances: he wished there were somebody there who knew him and could nod to him. Nevertheless, he was spoken to, asked questions about various of his fellow countrymen, and made at home. Presently, however, an elderly member who had been silent and whom I will designate as being of the Dr. Samuel Johnson type, said:

"You seem to be having trouble in your packing houses over in America?"

We were.

"Very disgraceful, those exposures."

They were. It was May, 1906.

"Your Government seems to be doing something about it. It's certainly scandalous. Such abuses should never have been possible in the first place. It oughtn't to require your Government to stop it. It shouldn't have started."

"I fancy the facts aren't quite so bad as that sensational novel about Chicago makes them out," said the American. "At least I have been told so."

"It all sounds characteristic to me," said the Sam Johnson. "It's quite the sort of thing one expects to hear from the States."

"It is characteristic," said the American. "In spite of all the years that the sea has separated us, we're still inveterately like you, a bullying, dishonest lot—though we've had nothing quite so bad yet as your opium trade with China."

The Sam Johnson said no more.

At a ranch in Wyoming were a number of Americans and one Englishman, a man of note, bearing a celebrated name. He was telling the company what one could do in the way of amusement in the evening in London.

"And if there's nothing at the theatres and

everything else fails, you can always go to one of the restaurants and hear the Americans eat.''

There you have them, my anecdotes. They are chosen from many. I hope and believe that, between them all, they cover the ground; that, taken together as I want you to take them after you have taken them singly, they make my several points clear. As I see it, they reveal the chief whys and wherefores of friction between English and Americans. It is also my hope that I have been equally disagreeable to everybody. If I am to be banished from both countries, I shall try not to pass my exile in Switzerland, which is indeed a lovely place, but just now too full of celebrated Germans.

Beyond my two early points, the right to privacy and the mother-tongue, what are the generalizations to be drawn from my data? I should like to dodge spelling them out, I should immensely prefer to leave it here. Some readers know it already, knew it before I began; while for others, what has been said will be enough. These, if they have the will to friendship instead of the will to hate, will get rid of their anti-English complex, supposing that they had one, and understand better in future what has not been clear to them before. But I seem to feel that some readers there may be who will wish me to be more explicit.

First, then. England has a thousand years of greatness to her credit. Who would not be proud of that? Arrogance is the seamy side of pride. That is what has rubbed us Americans the wrong way. We are recent. Our thousand years of greatness are to come. Such is our passionate belief. Crudity is the seamy side of youth. Our crudity rubs the English the wrong way. Compare the American who said we were going to buy England for a summer resort with the Englishman who said that when all other entertainment in London failed, you could always listen to the Americans eat. Crudity, ''freshness'' on our side, arrogance, toploftiness on theirs: such is one generalization I would have you disengage from my anecdotes.

Second. The English are blunter than we. They talk to us as they would talk to themselves. The way we take it reveals that we are too often thin-skinned. Recent people are apt to be thin-skinned and self-conscious and self-assertive, while those with a thousand years of tradition would have thicker hides and would never feel it necessary to assert themselves. Give an Englishman as good as he gives you, and you are certain to win his respect, and probably his regard. In this connection see my anecdote about the Tommies and Yankees who physically fought it out, and compare it with the Salisbury, the van Squibber, and the opium trade anecdotes. "Treat 'em rough," when they treat you rough: they like it. Only, be sure you do it in the right way.

Third. We differ because we are alike. That American who stood in the theatre complaining about the sixpence he didn't have to pay at home is exactly like Englishmen I have seen complaining about the unexpected here. We share not only the same mother-tongue, we share every other fundamental thing upon which our welfare rests and our lives are carried on. We like the same things, we hate the same things. We have the same notions about justice, law, conduct; about what a man should be, about what a woman should be. It is like the mother-tongue we share, yet speak with a difference. Take the mother-tongue for a parable and symbol of all the rest. Just as the word "girl" is identical to our sight but not to our hearing, and means oh! quite the same thing throughout us all in all its meanings, so that identity of nature which we share comes often to the surface in different guise. Our loquacity estranges the Englishman, his silence estranges us. Behind that silence beats the English heart, warm, constant, and true; none other like it on earth, except our own at its best, beating behind our loquacity.

Thus far my anecdotes carry me. May they help some reader to a better understanding of what he has misunderstood heretofore!

No anecdotes that I can find (though I am sure that they are to be found) will illustrate one difference between the two peoples, very noticeable to-day. It is increasing. An Englishman not only sticks closer than a brother to his own rights, he respects the rights of his neighbor just as strictly. We Americans are losing our grip on this. It is the bottom of the whole thing. It is the moral keystone of democracy. Howsoever we may talk about our own rights to-day, we pay less and less respect to those of our neighbors. The result is that to-day there is more liberty in England than here. Liberty consists and depends upon respecting your neighbor's rights every bit as fairly and squarely as your own.

On the other hand, I wonder if the English

are as good losers as we are? Hardly anything that they could do would rub us more the wrong way than to deny to us that fair play in sport which they accord each other. I shall not more than mention the match between our Benicia Boy and their Tom Sayers. Of this the English version is as defective as our school-book account of the Revolution. I shall also pass over various other international events that are somewhat well known, and I will illustrate the point with an anecdote known to but a few.

Crossing the ocean were some young English and Americans, who got up an international tug-of-war. A friend of mine was anchor of our team. We happened to win. They didn't take it very well. One of them said to the anchor:

"Do you know why you pulled us over the line?"

"No."

"Because you had all the blackguards on your side of the line."

"Do you know why we had all the blackguards on our side of the line?" inquired the American.

"No."

"Because we pulled you over the line."

In one of my anecdotes I used the term Sam
Johnson to describe an Englishman of a certain type. Dr. Samuel Johnson was a very
marked specimen of the type, and almost the
only illustrious Englishman of letters during
our Revolutionary troubles who was not our
friend. Right down through the years ever
since, there have been Sam Johnsons writing
and saying unfavorable things about us. The
Tory must be eternal, as much as the Whig
or Liberal; and both are always needed.
There will probably always be Sam Johnsons
in England, just like the one who was scandal-
ized by our Chicago packing-house dis-
closures. No longer ago than June 1, 1919,
a Sam Johnson, who was discussing the Peace
Treaty, said in my hearing, in London:

"The Yankees shouldn't have been brought
into any consultation. They aided and abetted
Germany."

In *Littell's Living Age* of July 20, 1918,
pages 151–160, you may read an interesting
account of British writers on the United
States. The bygone ones were pretty prepos-
terous. They satirized the newness of a new
country. It was like visiting the Esquimaux
and complaining that they grew no pineapples
and wore skins. In *Littell* you will find how

few are the recent Sam Johnsons as compared
with the recent friendly writers. You will
also be reminded that our anti-English complex was discerned generations ago by Washington Irving. He said in his *Sketch Book*
that writers in this country were "instilling
anger and resentment into the bosom of a
youthful nation, to grow with its growth and
to strengthen with its strength."

And he quotes from the English *Quarterly
Review,* which in that early day already wrote
of America and England:

"There is a sacred bond between us by
blood and by language which no circumstances can break. . . . Nations are too
ready to admit that they have natural enemies; why should they be less willing to believe that they have natural friends?"

It is we ourselves to-day, not England, that
are pushing friendship away. It is our politicians, papers, and propagandists who are
making the trouble and the noise. In England
the will to friendship rules, has ruled for a
long while. Does the will to hate rule with us?
Do we prefer Germany? Do we prefer the
independence of Ireland to the peace of the
world?

XVI

A PART of the Irish is asking our voice and our gold to help independence for the whole of the Irish. Independence is not desired by the whole of the Irish. Irishmen of Ulster have plainly said so. Everybody knows this. Roman Catholics themselves are not unanimous. Only some of them desire independence. These, known as Sinn Fein, appeal to us for deliverance from their conqueror and oppressor; they dwell upon the oppression of England beneath which Ireland is now crushed. They refer to England's brutal and unjustifiable conquest of the Irish nation seven hundred and forty-eight years ago.

What is the truth, what are the facts?

By his bull "Laudabiliter," in 1155, Pope Adrian the Fourth invited the King of England to take charge of Ireland. In 1172 Pope Alexander the Third confirmed this by several letters, at present preserved in the Black Book of the Exchequer. Accordingly, Henry the Second went to Ireland. All the archbishops and bishops of Ireland met him at Waterford, received him as king and lord of Ireland, vowing loyal obedience to him and his successors, and acknowledging fealty to them forever. These prelates were followed by the kings of Cork, Limerick, Ossory, Meath, and by Reginald of Waterford. Roderick O'Connor, King of Connaught, joined them in 1175. All these accepted Henry the Second of England as their Lord and King, swearing to be loyal to him and his successors forever.

Such was England's brutal and unjustifiable conquest of Ireland.

Ireland was not a nation, it was a tribal chaos. The Irish nation of that day is a legend, a myth, built by poetic imagination. During the centuries succeeding Henry the Second, were many eras of violence and bloodshed. In reading the story, it is hard to say which side committed the most crimes. During those same centuries, violence and bloodshed and oppression existed everywhere in Europe. Undoubtedly England was very oppressive to Ireland at times; but since the days of Gladstone she has steadily endeavored to relieve Ireland, with the result that to-day she is oppressing Ireland rather less than our Federal Government is oppressing Massachusetts, or South Carolina, or any State. By the Wyndham Land Act of 1903, Ireland was placed in a position so advantageous, so utterly the reverse of oppression, that Dillon, the present leader, hastened to obstruct the operation of the Act, lest the Irish genius for grievance might perish from starvation. Examine the state of things for yourself, I cannot swell this book with the details; they are as accessible to you as the few facts about the conquest which I have just narrated. Examine the facts, but even without examining them, ask yourself this question: With Canada, Australia, and all those other colonies that I have named above, satisfied with England's rule, hastening to her assistance, and with only Ireland selling herself to Germany, is it not just possible that something is the matter with Ireland rather than with England?

Sinn Fein will hear of no Home Rule. Sinn Fein demands independence. Independence Sinn Fein will not get. Not only because of the outrage to unconsenting Ulster, but also because Britain, having just got rid of one Heligoland to the East, will not permit another to start up on the West. As early as

August 25th, 1914, mention in German papers was made of the presence in Berlin of Casement and of his mission to invite Germany to step into Ireland when England was fighting Germany. The traffic went steadily on from that time, and broke out in the revolution and the crimes in Dublin in 1916. England discovered the plan of the revolution just in time to foil the landing in Ireland of Germany, whom Ireland had invited there. Were England seeking to break loose from Ireland, she could sue Ireland for a divorce and name the Kaiser as co-respondent. Any court would grant it.

The part of Ireland which does not desire independence, which desires it so little that it was ready to resist Home Rule by force in 1914, is the steady, thrifty, clean, coherent, prosperous part of Ireland. It is the other, the unstable part of Ireland, which has declared Ireland to be a Republic. For convenience I will designate this part as Green Ireland, and the thrifty, stable part as Orange Ireland. So when our politicians sympathize with an "Irish" Republic, they befriend merely Green Ireland; they offend Orange Ireland.

Americans are being told in these days that

they owe a debt of support to Irish independence, because the "Irish" fought with us in our own struggle for independence. Yes, the Irish did, and we do owe them a debt of support. But it was the Orange Irish who fought in our Revolution, not the Green Irish. Therefore in paying the debt to the Green Irish and clamoring for "Irish" independence, we are double crossing the Orange Irish.

"It is a curious fact that in the Revolutionary War the Germans and Catholic Irish should have furnished the bulk of the auxiliaries to the regular English soldiers; . . . The fiercest and most ardent Americans of all, however, were the Presbyterian Irish settlers and their descendants." *History of New York*, p. 133, by Theodore Roosevelt.

Next, in what manner have the Green Irish incurred our thanks?

They made the ancient and honorable association of Tammany their own. Once it was American. Now Tammany is Green Irish. I do not believe that I need pause to tell you much about Tammany. It defeated Mitchel, a loyal but honest Catholic, and the best Mayor of New York in thirty years. It is a despotism built on corruption and fear.

During our Civil War, it was the Green

Irish that resisted the draft in New York. They would not fight. You have heard of the draft riots in New York in 1862. They would not fight for the Confederacy either.

During the following decade, in Pennsylvania, an association, called the Molly Maguires, terrorized the coal regions until their reign of assassination was brought to an end by the detection, conviction, and execution of their ringleaders. These were Green Irish.

In Cork and Queenstown during the recent war, our American sailors were assaulted and stoned by the Green Irish, because they had come to help fight Germany. These assaults, and the retaliations to which they led, became so serious that no naval men under the rank of Commander were permitted to go to Cork. Leading citizens of Cork came to beg that this order be rescinded. But, upon being cross-examined, it was found that the Green Irish who had made the trouble had never been punished. Of this many of us had news before Admiral Sims in *The World's Work* for November, pages 63–64, gave it his authoritative confirmation.

Taking one consideration with another, it hardly seems to me that our debt to the Green Irish is sufficiently heavy for us to hinder

England for the sake of helping them and Germany.

Not all the Green Irish were guilty of the attacks upon our sailors; not all by any means were pro-German; and I know personally of loyal Roman Catholics who are wholly on England's side, and are wholly opposed to Sinn Fein. Many such are here, many in Ireland: them I do not mean. It is Sinn Fein that I mean.

In 1918, when England with her back to the wall was fighting Germany, the Green Irish killed the draft. Here following, I give some specific instances of what the Roman Catholic priests said.

April 21st. After mass at Castletown, Bear Haven, Father Brennan ordered his flock to resist conscription, take the sacrament, and to be ready to resist to the death; such death insuring the full benediction of God and his Church. If the police resort to force, let the people kill the police as they would kill any one who threatened their lives. If soldiers came in support of the draft, let them be treated like the police. Policemen and soldiers dying in their attempt to carry out the draft law, would die the enemies of God, while the people who resisted them would die in peace with God and under the benediction of his Church.

Father Lynch said in church at Ryehill: "Resist the draft by every means in your power. Any minion of the English Government who fires upon you, above all if he is a Catholic, commits a mortal sin and God will punish him."

In the chapel at Kilgarvan Father Murphy said: "Every Irishman who helps to apply the draft in Ireland is not only a traitor to his country, but commits a mortal sin against God's law."

At mass in Scariff the Rev. James MacInerney said: "No Irish Catholic, whatever his station be, can help the draft in this country without denying his faith."

April 28th. After having given the communion to three hundred men in the church at Eyries, County Cork, Father Gerald Dennehy said: "Any Catholic who either as policeman or as agent of the government shall assist in applying the draft, shall be excommunicated and cursed by the Roman Catholic Church. The curse of God will follow him in every land. You can kill him at sight, God will bless you and it will be the most acceptable sacrifice that you can offer."

Referring to any policeman who should attempt to enforce the draft, Father Murphy said at mass in Killenna, "Any policeman who is killed in such attempt will be damned in hell, even if he was in a state of grace that very morning."

Ninety-five percent of those Irish policemen were Catholics and had to respect the commands of those priests.

Ireland is England's business, not ours. But the word "self-determination" appears to hypnotize some Americans. We must not be hypnotized by this word. It is upon the "principle" expressed in this word that our sympathies with the Irish Republic are asked. The six northeastern counties of Ulster, on the "principle" of self-determination, should be separated from the Irish Republic. But the Green Irish will not listen to that. Protestants in Ulster had to listen in their own chief city to Sinn Fein rejoicings over German victories. The rebellion of 1916, when Sinn Fein opened the back door that England's enemies might enter and destroy her—this dastardly treason was made bloody by cowardly violence. The unarmed and the unsuspecting were shot down and stabbed in cold blood. Later, soldiers who came home from the front, wounded soldiers too, were persecuted and assaulted. The men of Ulster don't wish to fall under the power of the Green Irish.

"We do not know whether the British statesmen are right in asserting a connection between Irish revolutionary feeling and German propaganda. But in such a connection we should see no sign of a bad German policy." Thus wrote a Prussian deputy in *Das Grössere Deutschland.* That was over there. This was over here:—

"The fraternal understanding which unites the Ancient Order of Hibernians and the German-American Alliance receives our unqualified endorsement. This unity of effort in all matters of a public nature intended to circumvent the efforts of England to secure an Anglo-American alliance have been productive of very successful results. The congratulations of those of us who live under the flag of the United States are extended to our German-American fellow citizens upon the conquests won by the fatherland, and we assure them of our unshaken confidence that the German Empire will crush England and aid in the liberation of Ireland, and be a real defender of small nations." See the *Boston Herald* of July 22, 1916.

During our Civil War, in 1862, a resolution of sympathy with the South was stifled in Parliament.

On June 6, 1919, our Senate passed, with one dissenting voice, the following, offered by Senator Walsh, Democrat, of Massachusetts:

"Resolved, that the Senate of the United States express its sympathy with the aspirations of the Irish people for a government of its own choice."

What England would not do for the South in 1862, we now do against England our ally, against Ulster, our friend in our Revolution, and in support of England's enemies, Sinn Fein and Germany.

Ireland has less than 4,500,000 inhabitants; Ulster's share is about one third, and its Protestants outnumber its Catholics by more than three fourths. Besides such reprisals as they saw wrought upon wounded soldiers, they know that the Green Irish who insist that Ulster belong to their Republic, do so because they plan to make prosperous and thrifty Ulster their milch cow.

Let every fair-minded American pause, then, before giving his sympathy to an independent Irish Republic on the principle of self-determination, or out of gratitude to the Green Irish. Let him remember that it was the Orange Irish who helped us in our Revolution, and that the Orange Irish do not want an independent Irish Republic. There will be none; our interference merely makes Germany happy and possibly prolongs the existing chaos; but there will be none. Before such loyal and thinking Catholics as the gentleman who said to me that word about ''spoiling the ship for a ha'pennyworth of tar,'' and before a firm and coherent policy on England's part, Sinn Fein will fade like a poisonous mist.

XVII

SOLDIERS of ours—many soldiers, I am sorry to say—have come back from Coblenz and other places in the black spot, saying that they found the inhabitants of the black spot kind and agreeable. They give this reason for liking the Germans better than they do the English. They found the Germans agreeable, the English not agreeable. Well, this amounts to something as far as it goes: but how far does it go, and how much does it amount to? Have you ever seen an automobile painted up to look like new, and it broke down before it had run ten miles, and you found its insides were wrong? Would you buy an automobile on the strength of the paint? England often needs paint, but her insides are all right. If our soldiers look no deeper than the paint, if our voters look no further than the paint, if our democracy never looks at anything but the paint, God help our democracy! Of course the Germans were agreeable to our soldiers *after the armistice!*

Agreeable Germany!—who sank the *Lusitania;* who sank five thousand British merchant ships with the loss of fifteen thousand men, women, and children, all murdered at sea, without a chance for their lives; who fired on boat-loads of the shipwrecked, who stood on her submarine and laughed at the drowning passengers of the torpedoed *Falaba.*

Disagreeable England!—who sank five hundred German ships without permitting a single life to be lost, who never fired a shot until provision had been made for the safety of passengers and crews.

Agreeable Germany!—who, as she retreated, poisoned wells and gassed the citizens from whose village she was running away; who wrecked the churches and the homes of the helpless living, and bombed the tombs of the helpless dead; who wrenched families apart in the night, taking their boys to slavery and their girls to wholesale violation, leaving the old people to wander in loneliness and die; who in her raids upon England slaughtered three hundred and forty-two women, and killed or injured seven hundred and fifty-seven children, and made in all a list of four thousand five hundred and sixty-eight, bombed by her airmen; whose trained nurses met our wounded and captured men at the railroad trains and held out cups of water for them to see, and then poured them on the ground or spat in them.

Disagreeable England!—whose colonies rushed to help her: Canada, who within eight weeks after war had been declared, came with a voluntary army of thirty-three thousand men; who stood her ground against that first meeting with the poison gas and saved not only the day, but possibly the whole cause; who by 1917 had sent over four hundred thousand men to help disagreeable England; who gave her wealth, her food, her substance; who poured every symbol of aid and love into disagreeable England's lap to help her beat agreeable Germany. Thus did all England's colonies offer and bring both themselves and their resources, from the smallest to the greatest; little Newfoundland, whose regiment gave such heroic account of itself at Gallipoli; Australia who came with her cruisers, and with also her armies to the West Front and in South Africa; New Zealand who came from the other side of the world with men and money—three million pounds in gift, not loan, from one million people. And the Boers? The Boers, who latest of all, not twenty years be-

fore, had been at war with England, and conquered by her, and then by her had been given
a Boer Government. What did the Boers do?
In spite of the Kaiser's telegram of sympathy, in spite of his plans and his hopes, they
too, like Canada and New Zealand and all the
rest, sided of their own free will with disagreeable England against agreeable Germany. They first stamped out a German rebellion, instigated in their midst, and then
these Boers left their farms, and came to
England's aid, and drove German power from
Southwest Africa. And do you remember the
wire that came from India to London? "What
orders from the King-Emperor for me and
my men?" These were the words of the
Maharajah of Rewa; and thus spoke the rest
of India. The troops she sent captured Neuve
Chapelle. From first to last they fought in
many places for the Cause of England.

What do words, or propaganda, what does
anything count in the face of such facts as
these?

Agreeable Germany!—who addresses her
God, "Thou who dwellest high above the
Cherubim, Seraphim and Zeppelin"—Parson
Diedrich Vorwerck in his volume *Hurrah and
Hallelujah*. Germany, who says, "It is better

to let a hundred women and children belonging to the enemy die of hunger than to let a single German soldier suffer''—General von der Goltz in his *Ten Iron Commandments of the German Soldier;* Germany, whose soldier obeys those commandments thus: "I am sending you a ring made out of a piece of shell. . . . During the battle of Budonviller I did away with four women and seven young girls in five minutes. The Captain had told me to shoot these French sows, but I preferred to run my bayonet through them''—private Johann Wenger to his German sweetheart, dated Peronne, March 16, 1915. Germany, whose newspaper the Cologne *Volkszeitung* deplored the doings of her *Kultur* on land and sea thus: "Much as we detest it as human beings and as Christians, yet we exult in it as Germans."

Agreeable Germany!—whose Kaiser, if his fleet had been larger, would have taken us by the scruff of the neck.

"Then Thou, Almighty One, send Thy lightnings!
Let dwellings and cottages become ashes in the heat of fire.
Let the people in hordes burn and drown with wife and child.
May their seed be trampled under our feet;
May we kill great and small in the lust of joy.
May we plunge our daggers into their bodies,
May Poland reek in the glow of fire and ashes.''

· That is another verse of Germany's hymn,
hate for Poland; that is her way of taking
people by the scruff of the neck; and that is
what Senator Walsh's resolution of sympathy
with Ireland, Germany's contemplated Heligoland, implies for the United States, if Germany's deferred day should come.

XVIII

NATIONS do not like each other. No
plainer fact stares at us from the
pages of history since the beginning.
Are we to sit down under this forever? Why
should we make no attempt to change this for
the better in the pages of history that are yet
to be written? Other evils have been made
better. In this very war, the outcry against
Germany has been because she deliberately
brought back into war the cruelties and the
horrors of more barbarous times, and with
cold calculations of premeditated science
made these horrors worse. Our recoil from
this deed of hers and what it has brought upon
the world is seen in our wish for a League of
Nations. The thought of any more battles,
trenches, submarines, air-raids, starvation,
misery, is so unbearable to our bruised and
stricken minds, that we have put it into words
whose import is, Let us have no more of this!
We have at least put it into words. That such
words, that such a League, can now grow into

something more than words, is the hope of many, the doubt of many, the belief of a few. It is the belief of Mr. Wilson; of Mr. Taft; Lord Bryce; and of Lord Grey, a quiet Englishman, whose statesmanship during those last ten murky days of July, 1914, when he strove to avert the dreadful years that followed, will shine bright and permanent. We must not be chilled by the doubters. Especially is the scheme doubted in dear old Europe. Dear old Europe is so old; we are so young; we cause her to smile. Yet it is not such a contemptible thing to be young and innocent. Only, your innocence, while it makes you an idealist, must not blind you to the facts. Your idea must not rest upon sand. It must have a little rock to start with. The nearest rock in sight is friendship between England and ourselves.

The will to friendship—or the will to hate? Which do you choose? Which do you think is the best foundation for the League of Nations? Do you imagine that so long as nations do not like each other, that mere words of good intention, written on mere paper, are going to be enough? Write down the words by all means, but see to it that behind your words there shall exist actual

good will. Discourage histories for children
(and for grown-ups too) which breed international dislike. Such exist among us all. There
is a recent one, written in England, that needs
some changes.

Should an Englishman say to me:

"I have the will to friendship. Is there any
particular thing which I can do to help?" I
should answer him:

"Just now, or in any days to come, should
you be tempted to remind us that we did not
protest against the martyrdom of Belgium,
that we were a bit slow in coming into the
war,—oh, don't utter that reproach! Go back
to your own past; look, for instance, at your
guarantee to Denmark, at Lord John Russell's words: 'Her Majesty could not see with
indifference a military occupation of Hol-
stein'—and then see what England shirked;
and read that scathing sentence spoken to her
ambassador in Russia: 'Then we may dismiss
any idea that England will fight on a point of
honor.' We had made you no such guarantee.
We were three thousand miles away—how far
was Denmark?

"And another thing. On August 6, 1919,
when Britain's thanks to her land and sea
forces were moved in both houses of Parlia-

ment, the gentleman who moved them in the House of Lords said something which, as it seems to me, adds nothing to the tribute he had already paid so eloquently. He had spoken of the greater incentive to courage which the French and Belgians had, because their homes and soil were invaded, while England's soldiers had suffered no invasion of their island. They had not the stimulus of the knowledge that the frontier of their country had been violated, their homes broken up, their families enslaved, or worse. And then he added: 'I have sometimes wondered in my own mind, though I have hardly dared confess the sentiment, whether the gallant troops of our Allies would have fought with equal spirit and so long a time as they did, had they been engaged in the Highlands of Scotland or on the marches of the Welsh border.' Why express that wonder? Is there not here an instance of that needless overlooking of the feelings of others, by which, in times past, you have chilled those others? Look out for that.''

And should an American say to me:

''I have the will to friendship. What can I personally do?'' I should say:

''Play fair! Look over our history from that Treaty of Paris in 1783, down through

the Louisiana Purchase, the Monroe Doctrine,
and Manila Bay; look at the facts. You will
see that no matter how acrimoniously England has quarreled with us, these were always
family scraps, in which she held out for her
own interests just as we did for ours. But
whenever the question lay between ourselves
and Spain, or France, or Germany, or any
foreign power, England stood with us against
them.

"And another thing. Not all Americans
boast, but we have a reputation for boasting.
Our Secretary of the Navy gave our navy the
whole credit for transporting our soldiers to
Europe when England did more than half
of it. At Annapolis there has been a poster,
showing a big American sailor with a doughboy on his back, and underneath the words,
'We put them across.' A brigadier general
has written a book entitled, *How the Marines
Saved Paris*. Beside the marines there were
some engineers. And how about M Company
of the 23d regiment of the 2d Division? It
lost in one day at Château-Thierry all its men
but seven. And did the general forget the 3d
Division between Château-Thierry and Dor-
mans? Don't be like that brigadier general,
and don't be like that American officer return-

ing on the *Lapland* who told the British at his table he was glad to get home after cleaning up the mess which the British had made. Resemble as little as possible our present Secretary of the Navy. Avoid boasting. Our contribution to victory was quite enough without boasting. The head-master of one of our great schools has put it thus to his schoolboys who fought: "Some people had to raise a hundred dollars. After struggling for years they could only raise seventy-five. Then a man came along and furnished the remaining necessary twenty-five dollars. That is a good way to put it. What good would our twenty-five dollars have been, and where should we have been, if the other fellows hadn't raised the seventy-five dollars first?"

XIX

MY task is done. I have discussed with as much brevity as I could the three foundations of our ancient grudge against England: our school textbooks, our various controversies from the Revolution to the Alaskan boundary dispute, and certain differences in customs and manners. Some of our historians to whom I refer are themselves affected by the ancient grudge. You will see this if you read them; you will find the facts, which they give faithfully, and you will also find that they often (and I think unconsciously) color such facts as are to England's discredit and leave pale such as are to her credit, just as we remember the *Alabama*, and forget the Lancashire cotton-spinners. You cannot fail to find, unless your anti-English complex tilts your judgment incurably, that England has been to us, on the whole, very much more friendly than unfriendly—if not at the beginning, certainly at the end of each controversy. What an anti-English complex can do in the face of 1914, is hard to imagine:

Canada, Australia, New Zealand, India, the Boers, all Great Britain's colonies, coming across the world to pour their gold and their blood out for her! She did not ask them; she could not force them; of their own free will they did it. In the whole story of mankind such a splendid tribute of confidence and loyalty has never before been paid to any nation.

In this many-peopled world England is our nearest relation. From Bonaparte to the Kaiser, never has she allowed any outsider to harm us. We are her cub. She has often clawed us, and we have clawed her in return. This will probably go on. Once earlier in these pages, I asked the reader not to misinterpret me, and now at the end I make the same request. I have not sought to persuade him that Great Britain is a charitable institution. What nation is, or could be, given the nature of man? Her good treatment of us has been to her own interest. She is wise, far-seeing, less of an opportunist in her statesmanship than any other nation. She has seen clearly and ever more clearly that our good will was to her advantage. And beneath her wisdom, at the bottom of all, is her sense of our kinship through liberty defined and assured by law. If we were so far-seeing as she is, we also should know that her good will is equally important to us: not alone for material reasons, or for the sake of our safety, but also for those few deep, ultimate ideals of law, liberty, life, manhood and womanhood, which we share with her, which we got from her, because she is our nearest relation in this many-peopled world.

Lightning Source UK Ltd.
Milton Keynes UK
UKOW04f0808280915

259388UK00001B/127/P

9 781434 490384